the lecture

Lydie Salvayre

Translation by Linda Coverdale

Dalkey Archive Press
Normal · London

First published in French as *La Conférence de Cintegabelle* by Éditions du Seuil/Éditions Verticales, 1999
Copyright © 1999 by Lydie Salvayre
Translation © 2005 by Linda Coverdale

First edition, 2005

Library of Congress Cataloging-in-Publication Data:

Salvayre, Lydie, 1948–
    [Conférence de Cintegabelle. English]
    The lecture / by Lydie Salvayre ; translation by Linda Coverdale.— 1st Dalkey Archive ed.
        p. cm.
    ISBN 1-56478-351-0 (alk. paper)
    I. Coverdale, Linda. II. Title.

PQ2679.A52435C6713 2005
843'.914—dc22

                                                                2004063482

*Ouvrage publié avec le concours du
Ministère français chargé de la Culture – Centre National du Livre.*
[This Work has been published thanks to the
French Ministry of Culture – National Book Center.]

Partially funded by grants from the National Endowment for the Arts,
a federal agency, and the Illinois Arts Council, a state agency.

Dalkey Archive Press is a nonprofit organization located at
Milner Library (Illinois State University) and distributed in the UK
by Turnaround Publisher Services Ltd. (London).

www.dalkeyarchive.com

Printed on permanent/durable acid-free paper and bound in the
United States of America.

and do not blush at the thought
of what is the human heart.

Lautréamont, *The Songs of Maldoror*

Take a French dinner party. In Paris. Chez Armand. A chic dinner. The kind I don't go to. Pearls, crystal, the works.

Observe the guests. Scientifically. They turn to the left and right. Shake their heads. Gesture repeatedly with their right arms in a manner known as pronation. Devote themselves to mastication, mouths closed, I should add. And between two tiny mouthfuls, I should add, they move their lips constantly. Like this.

Because for them, ladies and gentlemen, conversation has replaced everything else. They neither laugh nor belch. Belching went out of fashion with regicide. That's the remark my brother-in-law made just to mortify me. At the table. In front of everyone. The day of the funeral. As I was choking back a hiccup between two sobs.

In the time of the Bourbon Louis, he announced with ludicrous pedantry, there was an official called the hastener who was in charge of the king's belches. Sometimes the king's belch was slow in coming, and all the courtiers would wring their hands, quiver with impatience, and turn sorrowful countenances toward the royal valve: But let him hasten, then, let this hastener hasten the sacred belch of the king! The hastener and his king have been done away with. And belchery with them. Those are great losses indeed.

Still, I thought, not so great as Lucienne's death. Forgive me, but my grief is as fresh, if I may say so, as a vegetable. I said vegetable. I really shouldn't have. That's the word I often use to evoke her, so calm, so—how shall I put it—so superbly lumpish. But let us stifle our grief. And let us return to that dinner party with which I opened my lecture. We may conclude, from our thorough investigation, that while it is generally admitted that speech is the achievement of all mankind,

—

conversation is a specialty that is eminently French.

—

That is our first and most heartening axiom. A specialty, I emphasize this, that is not exportable. Because it is not merchandise. It is even quite the opposite. I shall come back to this essential point. At the proper time. With the methodical turn of mind that is my wont.

We French, I was saying, are champions at conversation. This distinguishing trait, long elevated to the status of a national virtue, made the reputation of France and secured its reign.

Well, that art at which we excel is today in peril. I am sounding the alarm in our little town in hopes of alerting the highest authorities. Mediocrity, ladies and gentlemen, is going international. The fear of offending prevails more and more over the taste for talking. A generous spirit is discredited, if not condemned outright. It is taken for weakness of intellect. From one end of the planet to the other, conversations are all the same. Their poverty of ideas is now in fashion. And their insipidness is sickening.

—

Conversation is going downhill.

—

That will be our second and most distressing axiom. We live, increasingly, without talking to one another. Is no life, then, worth the telling? We live without talking to one another and soon we will live without living, which gives me the shivers.

Conversation is going downhill and the country with it, they go hand in hand. And it is greatly to be feared, if nothing is done, that they will both wind up in the garbage. The vultures will finish the job. You can count on them.

So here, dear ladies and gentlemen of Cintegabelle, is my rescue plan, conceived in the utmost urgency and which I unhesitatingly declare to be of national utility, since by proposing to restore the luster of speech in the eyes of a world that has forgotten how to speak, it aims at nothing less than the civic renewal of our country and the polishing of its image so that, I'm catching my breath, so that, strong in its recovered prestige, the France of tomorrow may assure throughout the world the civilizing mission that has fallen to her from time immemorial. Might I ask you, children, to please stop snickering. And to stop moving your chairs around. It's irritating.

The subtle art of conversation, however—to which, I venture to say, I have devoted my genius—offers, aside from that patriotic virtue I have just mentioned, other advantages no less excellent albeit less directly civic. And which to my astonishment have not yet been the object of any detailed study.

The first of these advantages is that conversation is very useful for seducing women.

The second is that it's even handier for succeeding in society.

The third and most surprising is that in bringing joy to mankind, it contributes appreciably to reducing the deficit of the National Health Service. A subject of satisfaction for our government.

In the interest of clarity, my lecture will scrupulously observe each step of the following outline, which I ask you to please keep in mind.

Part One: The advantages of conversation, already noted, and upon which we will elaborate with a most mathematical rigor.

Part Two: Those conditions favorable to the flowering of conversation, which are ten in number:

—the presence of at least two persons;

—the comfort of the derrière;

—the ability to keep silent;

—courtesy;

—clarity;

—jocularity;

—the principle of equality;

—a sense of proportion;

—an insouciant disregard for time;

—freedom.

Part Three: Five examples of conversation selected from among the most common categories:

—amorous conversation;

—literary conversation;

—political conversation;

—patriotic conversation;

—conversation with the dead.

The whole thing enlivened by a number of axioms with which I am not at all displeased. I'm rather fond of axioms.

So, Part One: The advantages of conversation.

The first of the advantages of conversation, as I was saying, and not the least of them, is that conversation always finds remarkable favor with women. Every last one of them goes into raptures before a clever conversationalist, be he cross-eyed, pot-bellied, warty, a journalist, or deformed. Take me: noticeably ill-favored, with big ears, and a cowlick I spend hours plastering down, I was an immediate hit with Lucienne (a woman impervious to poetry and little given to linguistic acrobatics) the second I began to babble. And I must confess that my verbal vivacity and florid declarations (I commanded, at the time, a whole battery of tricks, classified by genre) did more to lift up her redoubtable skirt than any fumbling gesture I'd never have dared make anyway. I wasn't that stupid. And knew for a fact that

—

women's genitals communicate with their ears.

—

If, gentlemen—for it is to you, men of Cintegabelle, that I speak—if nevertheless you prove unable to resist the summons of the flesh, if you are seized with the desire to place your hand on the knee of an altogether too concupiscible woman, I urge you most emphatically: under no circumstances interrupt your harangue. Without ceasing to chatter, keep gaining ground. Advance stealthily and with ingratiating ploys. Like the sinuous serpent of desire. Pursue your reptation garlanded with pretty turns of phrase. In perfect synchrony, lay compliments at her feet and hands on her modesty. From poems to promises, from promises to prattle, you will proceed without mishap to the inevitable place. Once there, stop talking! Pounce!

The second advantage of conversation concerns in particular those scheming, bloodthirsty youths who crave a brilliant career in the Arts and Letters. You will find such young men everywhere, and our town is no exception.

That's right, my little wolf cubs in the first row, I'll have you know that you will achieve more through a funny remark, a turn of phrase, or a flash of wit than through your girlfriend's sex appeal, a complete familiarity with the twelve volumes of Quintilian's *De Institutione Oratoria*, and even the outstanding dishonesty that in France ranks demonstrably among the most important factors of success.

You see, I have a friend (who shall remain nameless), a regional writer, an expert on the arts and crafts of Languedoc, who, whenever he goes out in society, flounders, stammers, stares like an idiot at his perfectly ordinary shoes, and can only bleat "Ah" and "Oh" and "Uh" and sometimes "Hee-hee." Now, although each of these onomatopoeias contains a world of perplexity and terrifying apprehension, they do absolutely nothing to fuel the fires of literate conversation. As for the few times when this friend is invited to appear on a television program, it's just pitiful to hear him sputter away! Result:

he gets no name recognition, as the rabble say.

—

Lousy conversation is social suicide.

—

Through a quite common misunderstanding, his poor speaking skills make a poor impression on people, whose low opinion of him we find most unfair. But the world is made in such a way that

—

it is not enough to be talented,
one must also look the part.

—

This will be our inevitable axiom. The corollary to which is equally inevitable:

—

To appear to be what one is not is ridiculous,
like dressing up a monkey in a three-piece suit.

—

Or wearing one myself. The results are guaranteed. I am grotesque. Lucienne always told me so. She preferred me in a track suit. To my great sorrow. So it's better, it seems, to suit one's style to oneself. And what's more, one must know one's own style. And oneself. And how to make them work together. All that isn't easy. I feel I'm getting bogged down. Which happens whenever I try to think. I see no other way to land on my feet again (one couldn't dream up a more appropriate expression), no other way than to quote Baltasar Gracián, a philosopher whom I've discovered since my Lulu left me (mourning has its good points, you must admit).

When the bottom has fallen out of everything, this thinker wrote, nothing can replace it. And although you can spruce up what the English refer to as the "packaging" (it's me speaking now), try as you may to decorate the emptiness with ruffles, doll it up, swathe it in tissue paper, beribbon it with fancy words and frills, the emptiness stubbornly, imperturbably, remains. I will let you meditate a moment on what I've just said, before issuing the following warning.

Warning:

Whoever considers the subtle art of conversation simply a useful skill for social climbing is a fool and a cipher. For conversation presupposes, ladies and gentle-men (before swelling into chamber music, or jazz, or rock, depending), an incubation period when the riches of the mind ferment, I don't like that image because it reminds me of cheese, whereas, we'll get back to this, conversation is not a cheese, another French specialty along with champagne and the famous spirit of collabo-ration, and if we absolutely had to find a metaphor here, I'd propose that

—

conversation is a wine that improves with age.

—

Which means that in my eyes, it possesses every virtue. And not only does it not preclude either thought or cul-ture. Which are not acquired in one day. Or a hundred. Or a thousand. Lucienne, for example, barely attained their outer edges. And died as lightweight as the day she was born. I'm not speaking of her body, that poor shell, but of her soul, which had the thickness of a blotter. And not only, as I was saying, does conversation not preclude either thought or culture. It positively requires them.

Sanctifies them. And celebrates them. Just listen to me, for instance.

The preceding assertion might seem like a perfidious attack against certain modern writers whose profundity of thought and cultural capital—I love that last expression, simply saying it makes me feel rich, but not for long—whose cultural and more particularly syntactic capital is limited to pocket change. But God forbid we should wish them harm! Every poor man is our friend!

The third advantage of conversation, which we cannot emphasize enough because it has considerable consequences on both the personal and national levels, is that it brings joy.

Proof:

When the fears that keep people mute and mistrustful melt away, when their minds float along together and their thoughts soar like birds (isn't that lovely?), when—mysteriously—word joins with word, when sallies sally forth and laughter bubbles up (all things most rare, not to mention absurd, since our lives feature mostly the contrary), when people experience in speaking with one another the sweet sense of a common bond and a common love for the beautiful and the true, I did say a love for the beautiful and the true—and I have no intention of apologizing, forget it—a love for the beautiful and the true upon whose lips I bestow a trembling kiss, you heard me (and if cynics sneer, they'll really hear from me!), when, in short, people converse—they are happy, it's obvious.

—

To converse is sheer delight.
To forgo this pleasure is a great sin.

—

A few persons, among whom I am honored to count myself, still preserve this eccentricity from a bygone century, namely, the enjoyment of conversation, of honing, stimulating, fortifying, renewing, refreshing, reviving, inspiring, enlarging, and reclaiming the potentialities of their intelligence and the hidden resources of their *corazón*, a term I shall use henceforth to designate an organ that takes on its true symbolic dimension only in Spain. In a remote village by the name of Fatarella. Where Lucienne was born and died. I feel I am going to cry. January 2, 1999. Poor old woman! Without ever having known the pleasure of a conversation, what *I* call a conversation. Which presupposes, we shall see, a certain ability to construct sentences. What *I* call sentences. A subject, verb, and complement arranged in a grammatical fashion. Without ever knowing the pleasure of conversing, the effects of which, moreover, have been scandalously neglected by our major philosophers. For I am the first, and proud of it, the first to devote to these effects the study they richly merit and which will contribute, I have no doubt, to the history of human thought. I shall summarize my reflections on them with two consecutive lemmas, of which here is the most important.

—

The man content because he converses
is less wicked than the discontented man.

—

It's possible to verify this at any hour of the day at the checkout counters of a supermarket or in the streets of housing projects, to cite only two examples, among fifty, there are plenty to chose from, the wicked being, it would seem, much more enterprising than the rest of the population—now there's a subject I would like to explore: the unbelievable fecundity of the wicked, their fertile imaginations, their productive zeal and tireless enthusiasm, as compared to their ignorance and verbal impoverishment, a rather frequent combination, it would appear. And at the risk of seeming crazy and foolishly prophetic, I maintain, before the entire universe, that wars would break out less frequently if people conversed more frequently.

The second lemma is more modest, certainly, than the preceding one, but so what? And here goes nothing:

—

The man content because he converses
is less subject to illness than
the discontented man.

—

It is Dr. Anatole Jardin who established indisputably in May 1984 (an article published in No. 472 of *Science in Life*) that cancer develops preferentially in individuals suffering from a conversational deficit. Like my Lucienne. Who had at her disposal only about a hundred words. A hundred, utterly threadbare of course, especially the word *stomach*, which she pronounced at least ten times a day in accents of complaint, usually accompanied by the word *heaviness*, or *heartburn*, poor dumpling, plus the word *lotto*, which by the end had become an obsession. Dr. Jardin thus supplied a scientific foundation to something I had long suspected without ever putting it into words, still less into practice:

By giving human beings lofty things to think about, by diverting them from the frivolous claims of existence, by tearing them away from TV programs hosted by blonde bimbos, from patriotic soccer, from the spectacle of blood and other distractions in which they drown their sorrows, conversation notably increases the democratic tenor of their social consciousness, while at the same time distancing them from the torments of the hypochondria that results, as we know, from devoting too much attention to the internal organs.

From this last point, we may quite obviously conclude that

—

conversation appreciably reduces
the National Health Service deficit.

—

This is a great thing, for which other governments envy us.

But—for there is a but, and it's a big one—but conversation entails a major risk: it exposes stupidity in no time. That explains why the number of imbeciles seems higher in France than in other countries. Whereas it's roughly in the same range. In other words, considerable.

So my advice to you is:

If you feel the itch, young people, to express a few inept opinions (and that can happen to the loftiest minds), commit them to paper instead of voicing them. Write a novel, for example. Or a short essay. If a marketing-savvy publisher ever prints it, your nonsense will pass for thought. You will be a success. No longer will you have to worry about learning to converse. Because everyone forgives a winner everything. Even rank idiocy? Certainly. And wickedness? Absolutely. It's wonderful. Don't you agree?

Let's forge ahead. And move on to . . .

Part Two of our lecture.

To describe the manner and matter of human conversation would require considering France at every level, from top to bottom, and writing the nation's history, no more, no less.

I maintain in fact that a man's walk of life, be he ever so secretive, may be divined as—if not more—easily from his speech as from his dress, and that it is his most accurate, most merciless reflection, nay, that it is the man, the whole man, for all of him informs it and it shows all of him, for in it he conceals himself and in it he reveals himself. A serious subject if ever there was one, and the best possible source of information on the physiology of a country.

In elucidating the laws that govern Cintegabellian conversations, we will do no less, ladies and gentlemen, than embrace the whole of France. A presumptuous undertaking, some will say. A crackpot enterprise, will say others. With all due deference to small minds, we are devoted to the welfare of the Nation and prompted by the obliging intention to redress the wrongs done daily to this last square of survivors who, still taking themselves for men, still take it upon themselves to talk to one another, I know, it's laughable, and there's more hilarity to come, because we've got three or four old-fashioned ideas left to dig up and dust off, too bad if you're allergic, we are entirely devoted, we were saying, to our lovely land of France, thanks to which devotion this major speech will occupy in years to come its rightful place: the pinnacle.

But—a fig for personal satisfactions! Some of us, I see, are already growing impatient. Let's get right into this second part that will discuss, with much wit, the conditions necessary for the blossoming of a conversation.

First condition: To be more than one.

Since most people talk to themselves, it seems worthwhile to specify, ladies and gentlemen, that a conversation requires at least two people. At least two. That's why I was unable, conjugally speaking, to experience that delight: Lucienne and I, although quite different, were as one. Different, I said, especially in volume (quite unequally distributed between us), but love laughs at differences, doesn't it? Two people, therefore, at best, and ten at most. Beyond that, conversation degenerates into what is called, so aptly, a brouhaha, a word formed from the onomatopoeia Ha, which may be considered, in a social gathering, as the zero point of chitchat, even though it lends itself to endless permutation: Ha? Ha! Ha ha? Ha ha! Ha ha ha? Ha ha ha! Ha ha ha ha? Etc., etc.

Another requirement: people joining in conversation ought necessarily to select one another through reciprocal choice. This allows us to eliminate forthwith, from among the settings of causeries, the above-mentioned fashionable routs, those hotbeds of mutual dislike in the absence of mutual selection. It was Monsieur Whosis, Maître Hoare's legal secretary, who told me of the horrors he witnessed during the famous Saturday receptions, which were not, believe me, a pretty sight. Whence this aphorism, borrowed in part from a moralist of the seventeenth century whose complete works we purchased recently thanks to our modest capital.

—

It is the misfortune of nobodies
that they converse with nobody
of their own choosing.

—

My "nobodies" are still real people, you will notice, not phantoms. Why belabor a point, you'll say, that seems so obvious? Because our children—raised in an imaginary world, crazy about screens and virtual images—are in the process of forgetting these sacrosanct truths, to wit: firstly, that we consist of a body equipped with sensitive appendages (mine are particularly sensitive, and as for Lucienne's, let's not go there, they were nothing but open wounds, albeit paralyzed, my poor darling, I mean at the end, when she uttered prolonged, bestial moans, which I tried vainly to deaden by gagging her, but she didn't like that, the gag, I could tell from her staring eyes, so my only recourse was to blindfold her and murmur lovingly, Sleepy-time, my Lulu); secondly, that these sensitive appendages constantly affect our minds and our speech; and thirdly, that, deprived of conation, our minds and our speech dry up, wither away, and finally drop dead. Hence this indisputable axiom:

—

Conversation implies the activity of the senses
and the stimulus of sex.

—

It follows inevitably that the art of conversation will be forever inaccessible to:

those prone to cell-phone orgies and anxiety attacks;

travelers in the fourth dimension (who are not all interned in asylums);

cyberspacemen and other cruisers of information superhighways who never see or hear or hug one another.

All indications are that by jettisoning their bodies, these young websurfers whose sole surfboard is a brain of global dimensions, whose sole desire is a vague attraction to the tidal wave of shit that will engulf us all, whose sole passion is to brood before the blue of their screens, these youngsters on life-support sitting peacefully before their monitors while the world around them goes to hell in a handbasket, these young voyagers without hearts, nerves, muscles, without any defenses, without any formative experience of themselves or others, will finally, one of these centuries, disappear. I did say disappear. Just like the dinosaurs. I'd swear to it. And it saddens me. Because even though we have been pronounced obsolete, I am still attached to the human race that produced someone as delightful as my little cabbage—I called her my little cabbage, or Lulu, or my fatty, or my dear (not the four-legged one, the other), but usually my little cabbage, because she had the almost perfect roundness, vegetable immobility, and enigmatic beauty of a cabbage. And it is with a heavy heart that I make this dreadful prediction, which I am sure will have countless consequences:

—

The death of conversation heralds the death of Man.

—

This risk of extinction, which I am alone in formulating so bluntly, has led some to announce that I am nothing less than obsolete. Me, obsolete! I don't know what's keeping me from . . . but let's calm down. The wisest course is to pay no attention to such vile slander. Ladies and gentlemen, I'm telling you, I feel only contempt for those reactionaries who condemn progress and keep saying that the sky is falling. Personally, I love the future, I'm not kidding. I love the future the way I loved Lucienne. Passionately. Fearfully. Giddily.

And although I am well aware of the dangers of cybernetics, I must admit that it will transform the future in the most amazing fashion. By freeing us from the burden of our oh-so-earthly and ravenous and cumbersome bodies, cybernetics will liberate us from what we thought were the inescapable laws of gravity, in an incredible mutation that leads me to ask these concrete questions: will getting a hard-on be possible, and in what sense? Good Lord! And masturbation? And penetration? These, to my mind, are crucial questions that remain unanswered, yet at the same time it (I'm referring to cybernetics) will spare us the fainting spells, convulsions, itching, collusions, annoyances, chafing, secretions, and other disgusting things linked to incarnation. And believe me, I know what I'm talking about!

For my part, and despite the endless difficulties I encounter, endowed as I am with one hundred and thirty-two pounds of exquisitely sensitive flesh plus (I confess) a dreadfully tyrannical penis, I am still not resigned to becoming a pure spirit. Even on the Internet. But instead of anticipating the terrors to come, let us turn to the second condition:

The comfort of the derrière.

We have just evoked the corporeal presence of interlocutors, indispensable to any conversation. Let us now look closely at that most posterior part of the body, which has important—not to mention decisive—effects on the actions of the tongue. I wish to speak of the derrière.

Perspicacious as always, we have observed that the more comfortably a speaker is seated, the more elevated are his thoughts, gaining in quickness, liveliness, and charm, all valuable things for the art of conversation.

Contrariwise, we have not failed to notice that a glumly slouching ass, or a bony ass perched sadly on a mortifying iron chair, or even worse, an ass sorely martyred in the lotus position is often the cause of words as waspish as they are sullen and a poetic turn of pathetico-tragic inspiration that is truly deadly.

To convince you of this, we need merely study Rodin's *The Thinker,* who is seated, please note, on the narrowest of boulders. One can read in his face all the misery of his soul. Imagine him lounging in a comfy chair by the fire, on a luxurious bergère, or, quite simply, on a pouf: his face lights up immediately!

If we refer to our previously noted criteria, we can state here and now that the category of those unsuited to conversation includes:

Japanese sitting on hard tatami mats;

saints and martyrs whose pallets and seats are as inhospitable as their (I leave you to fill in the blanks);

and anyone whose spine is in incongruous motion—

I'm thinking of athletes, playboys, those engaged in fornication, pedestrians in a hurry, professors in mid-lecture, young ballet students, and all those engaged in arduous physical labor.

Other observations of equal sagacity have established that the amplitude of the derrière, the alleged seat of the soul—but dare we venture that far? I'm of two minds here—that the amplitude of the derrière also plays a decisive role in the brio of a conversation. In 1976, basing their study on the widely accepted fact that an emaciated ass reduced to two nubbins (I'm not revealing whose) is generally linked to the most paltry linguistic achievements, Brayeur and Hollarde brought to light the relationship between gluteal volume and amplitude of discourse.

There exist, however, exceptions to this rule. My Lucienne was one. Exception. For her backside was as wide as her speech was discreet. Discreet is the wrong word. Because the rare nouns at her disposal were bellowed. My Lulu poured such energy, such fervor, into everything! Idiot, she would bellow, poking fun at me. She liked to poke fun at me. We liked to poke fun at each other. From a sort of affectionate bashfulness. Fat blob, I'd riposte, delighting in the sight of her enormous posterior. You big cow, I'd say, while in my heart of hearts I called her my Callipygian Venus. But I shall not pursue this topic. I have no wish to weaken my credit through considerations you might find futile, nor to be reproached for neglecting the main point when my intention is precisely the opposite. For the moment I will simply summarize this chapter as follows:

From the perspective of both proclivity and circumference, the French, through their fundament, hold a privileged position in the world, which explains why they are champions in the conversational sphere:

primo, the majority show a marked predilection for the seated posture, a preference that leads many of them to choose a life-long position as a civil servant, in which post their conversation, slowly, turns to stone;

secundo, most of them possess rear ends of variable but always impressive amplitude, unlike Blacks and Yellows, whose gluteal diameter barely outstrips their cranial bisector.

If the government desires to revive a practice that, as we have said, encourages and strengthens good citizenship, and for which the French display the most gratifying predisposition, then we consider the authorities duty-bound—will they have the wisdom to listen to us?—to equip sundry buses, lanes, squares, and concourses with comfortable seats.

At the end of the lecture, I will pass around a petition in support of this project, in which I propose the purchase at reasonable prices of the couches of unemployed psychoanalysts, whose numbers, it seems, are on the rise in the big cities.

These couches will most advantageously replace our dull public benches. We shall not rest, my friends, until our project is carried out. For the moment, however, it has met with only a tepid reception from the Minister of Urban Affairs. Was he well or poorly seated when he reviewed my plan? That is the question. Which brings me, quite naturally, to offer you these two suggestions.

If you have an important decision to make, young ladies and gentlemen—for instance, on whether or not to marry—we urge you most emphatically to try the following approach. Mull over your options with your posterior planted on a soft sofa in the morning, and perched gingerly on the edge of some stone bench in the evening. This method has so far produced excellent results and prevented truly grievous disappointments. In marital matters. And other situations. I ought to know. Having decided to wed my Lucienne without taking the precautions I beg you to observe. Because I was at the time a complete sentimentalist. The songs of the teenage crooner Adamo pierced me to the heart, as did the sound of a guitar in the rustling night, pale water lilies nestled among reeds, billing and cooing in the moonlight, botched poetry and shivering hands—all so much crap that pitches you headfirst into endless disillusionment. Am I saying that I regret my marriage? Well, I . . . But let's set aside these much too intimate questions and return, ladies and gentlemen, to our main topic. I'm referring to conversation.

Before conversing, remember to equip yourselves with cigars, cigarettes, women, whisky, hashish, and other modern stimulants. They prove to be powerful aids to the art of speaking, for they all possess that incomparable albeit mysterious virtue of fostering the feeling that our earth is less awful than usual, and the pedestrians perambulating it, less frantic.

—

Bonum vinum laetificat cor hominis.

—

All those who disdain the pleasures of the aforenamed beverages and substances in the name of a suspect concern for their own health cannot in any way rise to the art of conversation. Drinkers of mineral water will be the first to go! They've been warned!

Third condition: The ability to keep silent.

I am in no way indulging in paradox when I assert that the third condition man requires for conversation is knowing how to keep quiet. Example. You can't beat examples. Especially personal examples. Example.

Lucienne and I happen to be in the kitchen. Before she fell into a coma. When she was still in full bloom.

I am in a philosophical mood. She is eating.

33

I am talking nonsense. She butters her bread.

I launch into a cloud of abstractions. She stuffs in her fifth slice.

I address her directly. She continues her methodical gorging.

But the silence gleaming in her gaze summons and encourages the rich profusion of my words. Extempore, I retrace the history of French literature, it's my pet subject. Sucking on my pipe, I've reached Julien Gracq and his anti-consumerism lampoon entitled *Literature: A Kick in the Stomach*. At that single word *stomach*, Lulu sits up abruptly. Stomach? she cries, and now it's her turn to soliloquize, wrenching me from the solipsistic limbo into which I'd been sinking.

That, my friends, is what a conversation is: that inability to tear ourselves away from ourselves—then suddenly, those words from someone else that touch us deeply and continue their charmed progression within us. What moral can we draw from this anecdote? I think I see one. It's that

—

in conversation, to speak and to be silent
are one and the same thing.

—

I bestow my silence upon someone who bestows his
speech upon me and those two movements add up, mag-
nifying and ennobling one another. But here I am, starting in with my big words again. For I have this ridiculous
quirk, I love big words. I love big words when they mean
big things. At the moment, the word *bestow*, which sends
me back to the word *Lulu*—you always wind up going
back to what you love: my Lulu, who possessed that uncommon generosity of offering me her silence, for entire
days, a silence barely broken by her masticatory grinding
and faint belching.

Bestowing silence, that's soon said, you'll tell me, and
on a blank page, it seems as poetic as can be. Bestowing,
but how? Since silence has vanished from our brains
(except from yours, my sleeping one, now silenced forever) and a deafening uproar pervades our sky.

Now we have reached the lofty question of the distinction between conversation, that lily of the soul, and

communication, that foul dunghill. A distinction that is starting to become, pardon my bluntness, a *pons asino- rum,* an ass's bridge that anyone but a fool can cross. So many treatises have tackled this theme that I hardly need mention it. Still, let me just whisper, my children, that silence is the essence of a conversation, its sister, its heaven, its great beyond, its promenade, its breath, its mystery, I'm waxing elegiac with enthusiasm, its sigh, its defeat, as well as its victory.

That is just about what I said, apart from the lyri- cism, to the owner of some firm or other whom I had the misfortune to run into last week and who was boasting to me about the extent of his "communications" busi- ness, I hate to say that word. I objected syllogistically to him that, one: the relentless assault of mass discourse on our defenseless ears was well on its way to exterminating silence; two: as a participant in the manufacture of said mass discourse, he was, three: neither more nor less than an exterminator. It was a serious accusation. A "self- made man," as the English say, he reacted coolly. What should he do, he asked me, always on the lookout for an angle. Like Gandhi, remain silent one day a week, I told him, or for even a few hours, indeed even a minute, as we do in memory of the dead (I mean the prominent dead, the others can go hang themselves, so to speak, my poor darling!), remain silent for a specified time, that's the solution, I exclaimed, if we don't want to keel over with our heads full of furor. The concept immediately inspired my businessman, who began to dream about great halls where silence would be, guess what, for sale. Amazing, I said. Especially since it's golden, I said. And can fetch a tidy sum. And as I burst out laughing, he replied, piqued, that he was quite serious about his idea. I laughed a little longer, but I was forcing it. That very evening, I wrote on the wall of night:

—

Silence is the courtesy of the soul.

—

Which seems to me a clever way, ladies and gentlemen, to bring you to the fourth condition:

Courtesy.

Allow me to take a sip of water.

Courtesy. Very important, courtesy. Primordial, I'd even say.

Examples.

My friend, the local writer of whom I spoke earlier, strikes up a conversation in an airport waiting room with a young woman who is rather pretty despite her acne. After five minutes, she wants to know everything there is to know about him and manages, as the expression goes, to worm his secrets out of him. The happiness of my friend, who can't stand worms or anyone prying into his life, evaporates in an instant. Politely, he takes his leave of the young woman. Which leads us to formulate this definitive axiom:

—

Any man of conversation, when asked a question that is indiscreet, beats an immediate retreat.

—

A man of my acquaintance calls his wife Pudgy-Wudgy in public. The unfortunate woman confides to anyone who will listen that she'd rather her husband slapped her instead of using that awful nickname.

Both husband and wife show a singular lack of the most elementary courtesy. What I mean is that neither of them has the slightest sense of distances. Because it is precisely courtesy that determines the exact distance between the slap, which moves us too far from its sender, and the nickname, which moves us too close. Or, to define courtesy in more general terms, it is what governs the physical as well as the symbolic separation between us and others, so that their words reach our ears without wafting any bad breath to our noses.

Although this distance protects us against exhalations and other miasmas engendered by promiscuity, nevertheless, it should not give us leave to neglect our personal hygiene. Whence this series of axioms that I submit to your judgment.

—

For pity's sake, ladies and gentlemen, overcome your fear of bathing. Avoid burping as well as passing gas. Despite the evident bliss thus procured. In an important conversation, being odorless is a plus. Better, use just a touch

39

of perfume. Eau de toilette is not made for dogs. Keep in mind that you should be pleasing to nostrils as well as to eyes and ears.

—

Refrain from interrupting a conversation by pointing at a turd or someone who reminds you, who knows why, of its oblong shape.

—

If you are invited to a dinner party, do not wipe your hands on the tablecloth, as my Lucienne did, finding that only natural, poor lamb. The code of good manners is incomprehensible, it's true, but one must know how to observe it. You find the chicken too salty? Do not go rinse it in lukewarm water. The French, in matters culinary, are extremely sensitive. Finally, you had best not clamp your cell phone to your mouth. That is just as rude as drinking from a bottle.

—

When tormented by a mediocre poet reading his verse aloud, learn to yawn through your nose. This little breathing exercise will keep you awake. And if you feel the onset of uncontrollable laughter, think of General Augusto Pinochet. It's foolproof.

—

Do not shout your opinions like a carnival barker. The man of conversation has a horror of right angles and rectangular thoughts. And if we had to find a mathematical figure for conversation, we would opt, without hesitation, for the tangent. Take a wall, for example. Try to speak to it face to face. The guardians of this wall will immediately suspect you of the worst things and will send you packing. Conversely, approach your wall at a tangent, in a slow stroll, and, with an innocent expression, slip a few words into its ear. The wall will be bowled over.

—

If you are determined to be a writer, do not dump your rubbish onto the paper as so many do. They have made the air of Paris unbreathable. I have personally confirmed this.

—

Do not guffaw in public simply at hearing the words *cunt prick balls* or *ass* the way my Lucienne did, who could no more hide her pleasure than her displeasure, the innocent dear. Hold your cackles until you can secretly indulge in the reading of contemporary novels, which abound in the items in question. I myself, moreover, sprinkled them around my speech in the typed version. People seem to like that sort of thing.

—

I will pass rapidly over those improprieties familiar, I would hope, to you all, such as the introduction of a finger into the nose or the obvious scratching of the pudenda. However humble your background, you will never be forgiven for such inconsiderate gestures.

—

If you feel like going hunting, imitate Confucius. Do not let fly at sleeping birds. Save your arrows for raptors. There are enough of them in France. You find my language too abstract? Certain names, naturally, spring to mind—but no. I will manage to contain myself. Whatever the cost. And will not overstep the bounds of the present speech. As I am often tempted to do.

—

Ladies and gentlemen, ever since the world began, no one would deny that the observance of the aforementioned taboos has spared mankind much unpleasantness. Many quarrels. And, let's say it, quite a few wars.

We deeply regret that certain boors do not consider themselves bound by this Charter of Courtesy. You would like to know what savage nation, what downtrodden country, what uncivilized and sanguinary tribe harbors these louts? It grieves me to distress you: these churls live in Cintegabelle, they have power, and crave even more. Heartless as well, devoid of elegance or integrity, they strive with extraordinary stubbornness to say neither Hello, nor Goodbye, nor Thank you, for fear of weakening their authority. Shame on these troglodytes who think themselves so grand. They would make us despair of the whole human race.

I will distress you even more if I ask you to add to this list of vulgarians the names of a few famous writers. Because, you must know by now, I recently met these remarkable people. Having gone up, as we say, to Paris, to present to our most eminent publishers the text of the lecture that you are the very first to hear, I received no fewer than seventeen rejections. Yet the grief this caused me was as nothing compared to that I felt upon returning home, where I found my Lucienne at death's door. My absence, on top of an alimentary deficiency (I'm the one who does the shopping) had dealt her the coup de grâce. I had in a way sacrificed her to my genius.

For I am a genius.

I place the things of the mind high above all others, and literature well above my Lucienne. This is the way of great men. That's what I explained to my Muse. My sacrificed Mumuse. Who had shrunk by about half. My little cabbage, I said to her, planting a kiss on her brow. My little Chinese cabbage, I added teasingly. But she lay motionless on her bed of pain, with contorted features, eyes rolled upwards, and not a trace of a smile. I sat down at her bedside and told her, glowing with pride, of my meetings with these remarkable people, writers. I spoke to her for hours without hearing a single grumble or protest, a wonderful memory! Some writers I had met, I confided to her, were quite affable, and I mentioned a few celebrated names without her snapping at me. Which should have warned me. But I was wholly absorbed in my joy at seeing her so rested, so welcoming, so marvelously subdued. Nevertheless, I said to her, taking advantage of her uncommon serenity to use an adverb that would normally have occasioned a burst of hilarity, since any unusual word used to make her die laughing, which always puzzled me, nevertheless, I told her, most of these writers, worn out by servile crawling (hard on the elbows and knees as well as the spirit), exhausted by wandering on paths of fame that are fraught, it seems, with myriad dangers, wind up plunged into the blackest misanthropy and behave, consequently, rather rudely. I expected a reaction from her. But . . . nothing. No reproach. No sarcasm. No tirade. A delicious calm. Which should have roused my suspicions. I blathered on like that for hours at her side, happier, in that meditative atmosphere, than I had been for ages. And it was not until quite late at night that I realized she was dying. Poor treasure. I feel that I . . . Excuse me.

Where were we? We were saying that among the remarkable people who are remarkable writers, there exist, remarkably, some who behave like swine. Your jaws drop? Pick them up. I haven't finished with the Philistines. And please add to this already lengthy list of clods the names of those dyed-in-the-wool revolutionaries, there are still some around, even in a town like ours, they're impossible to get rid of, you all know who I mean, who, fearing to be taken for dull bourgeois, vainly fling around foul language and coarse jokes, affecting the piggish behavior they imagine to be the mark of the common man.

They all deserve a thrashing!

A restrictive condition:

Courtesy, I postulated earlier, is an absolute requirement for conversation, but while its absence can be damaging, so can its excess.

Because by not discomfiting anyone and not dismissing any discourse, by always listening and replying amiably to anything, by thus seeming to approve of everything, one risks having no opinions whatsoever and looking like a jerk.

Ladies, gentlemen, my dear children: too many oratorical precautions, too many considerations, too many affectations, too many circumlocutions, too much pussyfooting around will muzzle your mouth, strangle your spirit, and force you to drivel perfect platitudes. Worse, you may end up effacing yourself, erasing yourself, I should say, before the mediocrity of Monsieur Tribulet and his ilk, at whom I myself dare to point a finger, no matter what peril may ensue.

Now, and this is of the highest importance, while it is necessary to speak one's mind politely, it is just as necessary to do so adequately.

Adequately, which means getting absolutely everything off one's chest, everything that feels heavy, as my Lucienne would say, were she to return from the great beyond, which is most unlikely, I won't allow myself in any case to hope for that, but you never know.

Adequately, which means following your train of thought to the end of the line, be it ever so unseemly and lead you to upset the apple cart—and I recall a few sublime instances of apple mayhem.

Adequately, I was saying, head high, shoulders back, spine straight. I feel as if I were describing a torero. Who converses, in a way, with his bull. But with his murderous intentions clearly proclaimed. Unlike the rest of us. More oblique. More devious. Less declarative.

Adequately, ladies and gentlemen, because once you bypass the thousand and one reasons for keeping your trap shut, to converse is to commit yourself, take risks, say who you are, insofar as you have any idea, I personally don't know anymore, I've been in a fog ever since losing my Lulu, who used to tell me who I was, so convenient, a good-for-nothing she'd say, the very definition of an artist, a good-at-nothing seems more like it to me, at *Nothing* with a capital N, for that touch of class.

But a plague on feelings! Enough about me! To converse, my young friends, is to take risks, to assert yourself, I was saying. Cowards, no doubt—who don't dare speak up except in front of their kids—cowards, no doubt, will misread this courage and call you arrogant or other slanderous epithets. I forbid you to defend yourselves!

And present you, to stiffen your resolve, with this well-thought-out axiom:

—

In a conversation, politeness ends
where malice begins.

—

This reduces the playing field considerably, let's face it. Monsieur Tribulet brims with indignation at your arguments! Well, let him choke on his indignation!

Monsieur Tribulet spews out his rotten hatred to your face! You have four solutions. Break off the conversation on the spot. Put the beast in his place, with his snout in his trough. Or advise him to shut up instanter. I've forgotten the fourth one.

Monsieur Tribulet, intoxicated with resentment, presses on despite your exhortations and utters scurrilities. Goodbye to courtesy and democratic considerations! Release your dogs! What am I saying? I'm losing the thread. The man of conversation never goes out with his dogs. Or his family. Monsieur Tribulet, I was saying, utters scurrilities. Now reinforce speech with ballistics, either in the form of insults fired off point blank, or the more sober well-aimed kick in the pants. You may even shake the knave by the collar, and slap his face coming and going, all methods with the undeniable merit of immediately relieving your outrage.

Nota bene:

Anger at a mean or foolish person must never last longer than three minutes and forty-six seconds. After that, it makes you yourself either mean or foolish. The situation is different if your anger must confront mean people in league with fools—in short, a nation. We have not studied, in such a case, the ideal time limit of anger. We will simply note that to date, the last historic hissy fit aimed at fools and meanies organized into armed groups lasted from June 18, 1940, to May 7, 1945, or close to five years.

We have good reason to fear that the next fit of anger—and it won't be long now—will be bigger. People always say that: It won't be long now . . . And if the next one takes a century to get here? That would really annoy me. To die before the bad guys get their trouncing. Even if it's only a slap on the wrist.

Question:

Must we, in peacetime, forbid swine to speak, as certain firebrands strongly recommend? This problem has remained unsolved for centuries. Personally, I feel that such a course would serve only to demean us.

Fifth condition: Clarity.

Since we happen to be talking about swine, just imagine, there exist some very peculiar pigs, most unpleasant pigs, who speak gibberish, and proudly too, pigs afflicted with a nasty mania: they take pleasure in seeing their obscurities bewilder the common people. We'll call these pigs the amphigorics.

Under no circumstances would we include among their numbers those geniuses who, being far in advance of their times, are not understood by their contemporaries until thirty years after their deaths. Blessed be they in their celestial solitude!

But let us return to our amphigoric pigs. For fear of being confused with the common run of cretins, they exhaust themselves with abstruse language that Lucienne, more radical than I, used to call scumbaggery, a word she particularly cherished and vigorously tossed my way whenever I wandered off into the firmament of ideas (*ether* would be a better term, I'll leave it at that), forcing me each time to nosedive back to earth and scrape my abstractions against the harsh surface of reality, thank you my Lulu, my gold nugget of Peru, my diamond of Golconda, my pearl of the Indies. How great a debt I owe you! You always showed me, with your native crudeness, how absurd it was to ignore the temporal world. But today you are no longer here to tell me when a discourse, losing touch with the tangible, becomes impenetrable, and I find the guidelines in this business, my dear departed, rather difficult to pin down. And now that I must define the category of the amphigorics, I'm wavering in perplexity, it's irritating, especially for a lecturer of my quality. I will therefore simply mention the only amphigorics who are absolutely unmistakable, I mean those sleazy pedants of whom my brother-in-law is the paragon: psychiatrist-cum-psychoanalysts who usually practice in the heart of Paris.

We have proposed to the most socialist of our national authorities a reclamation program targeting these self-important windbags who, in making themselves inaccessible to other people, thereby become inaccessible to the truth, as our august philosopher Archbishop Fénelo so astutely remarked. The details of this utopian project must remain under wraps for now, but I will share with you the following advice:

If you really must play the snob, practice on your wife. She is, all things considered, paid for that. But for heaven's sake, don't make a spectacle of yourself.

Banish frills and furbelows from your discourse. They are nothing, please excuse me, but bluffing and whoring-around.

Leave no danger of obscurity in your language. Although God knows we're drawn to the darkness! Myself most of all. To my misfortune. But I struggle against it, I struggle.

In other words, and to use an expression my Lulu loved, don't try to pull that one! Fake profundity repels us and is among the two or three frauds we would like to combat with strokes of . . . with strokes of the pen, the only weapon we have, a lightweight arm, I admit, compared to the enemy's tanks.

Don't add to the general nonsense. It holds only too great a sway. Now there's a sentence I like. I'll have to use it again. Just slightly refurbished. In another treatise. I have three in the works. If the media fallout from this lecture—on both the national and international levels— leaves me any breathing room.

When will we finally accept, my dear friends, that the mystery, I don't like that word, there's something cheap about it, that the mystery is not lurking someplace behind man, where we must go ferret it out, but within man, as it is within his works. No need to complicate things!

The mystery of speech lies in its precision, not its obscurity. That axiom is heartfelt and well-expressed, but suddenly I have doubts about it. What's happening to me? Let's continue.

Do me the favor, my friends, of leaving to Tribulet all petty allusions, twisted insinuations, tortuous turns of phrase, and various forms of cant. The soundness of your thoughts should suffice to distinguish you from the common herd.

Express yourself openly and in that resolute tone characteristic of a great mind. Avoid evasions. (That's exactly the kind of stylistic flourish that reeks of artifice and that I try doggedly to discredit.) Don't mince words, even if you offend the bigots wreathed in blushing squeamishness and the timid virgins who use only language swathed in cotton. I am proud to call myself a man of conversation and of peace, but I have declared

open war on common prudery. I've got my work cut
out for me!

—

Conversation detests the color violet,
a bastardization of red.

—

I shall explain. Come to think of it, no. The man of
conversation has no need to explain what he means. As
far as I know, he isn't making a speech on television!

Call a derrière a derrière and a fuck-up a fuck-up.
You will thus shame Monsieur Tribulet for his dissem-
bling. And if Monsieur Tribulet, shocked to the core, ex-
claims that one must not, sweet Jesus, speak so plainly,
that there are some things, etc., then tell him, perfectly
calmly, that a nobody like him is called a nobody. Or
worse.

Speak clearly. If you tend to mumble, practice speaking
more and more quickly: Sally sells seashells by the sea-
shore. Actually, that advice is idiotic. And risks blemishing
my lecture, which I wish to be exemplary in every way. I

offered that tongue twister merely to distract you, for I was mentally preparing my segue to the sixth condition:

Jocularity.

Crybabies, curmudgeons, sourpusses and other grumps, tireless recriminators, bitter moralizers, wallowers in disaster, whiney artists who drown the dryness of your souls in floods of gush, sad-sack killjoys who think smiles and laughter are vulgarities best left to plebeians, avaunt! Away with you, moaning multitudes! Do not dampen our shirt-fronts with your tears. And go blow your noses!

We feel only disgust for the gray flies of neurosis who buzz about your sobs, your pus, and all your weeping wounds. And you who extort credit from the credulous with your gloomy philosophical airs, you who drape yourselves in mourning black to write funereal verse, hoping to sound profound, get out of here! We are men of wit, for whom you are nothing less than monsters. And we curse you! Repeatedly!

For, as you have realized, jocularity, my dear friends, is our formal attire. Our elegance. Our code of ethics.

But I can already hear the grousers grumbling. Jocularity! When his wife was laid to rest barely two months ago! When the world is in such a depressing state! When a global Chernobyl is right around the corner! When we're about to land, if racism keeps up this way, in general carnage!

Well, yes. We are extremely sorry to assure you that we shall manage to remain, in spite of our suffering, cheerful men. We shall not add our tears to the sobs of those who cry alone. We shall not bemoan our dreadful fate with sheepish bleating. We shall not howl with the wolves prowling our urban jungles. Me, it's simple: when I catch sight of a wolf, even the meekest among them, I take to my heels. That's just my nature. I prefer to howl in my room. With the radio on. Because sometimes, you see, ever since my Lucienne went away, I howl. Sometimes I am afraid, at night, without her, in whom I used to cuddle, I say "in" on purpose, because back when she was in the pink of health, when she felt frisky, she would lay imperious hands on me, enfolding me in her enormous arms and clamping me to her immense belly, with my cowlick at the level of her neck. I would then feel completely surrounded by her fragrant flesh—I did say "fragrant" and I'm keeping that word, having long ago cast off the stupid olfactory prejudices that deprive us of the most sensuous smells—I would feel surrounded, I was saying, by her strongly piss-scented flesh, lying peacefully among her folds, drowning in her dampness, consoled, blissful, tiny. I would almost drool like a baby. In fact, I think I might have. Peepee, never, don't get me wrong. But now that she's gone, I am afraid. Afraid of this world that will crash straight into a wall if I take my eyes off it for one second. So I keep my eyes open until it hurts and smile to placate disaster.

Keeping my eyes wide open come what may, and bowing and scraping to the void: these, ladies and gentlemen, are my modest gymnastics, and I can assure you that they're beefing up my soul, in a big way.

People say that I'm wrestling with the idea of death. Of course. But gracefully, admit it. People say I no longer believe in the heavens, and not much in men. It's true. But I love, madly, the colors of the former and the complexity of the latter, and I would have sold, two months ago, my soul for my Lulu, my Lulu, my Lulu, if I'd found a buyer, which was, I agree, hardly likely. So, what do you expect, I chuckle when those self-righteous prigs who reproached me only a moment ago for my carefree behavior, when those self-righteous prigs girded with the best of intentions now accuse me of:

driving today's youth to despair when I gently try to open their eyes;

being a nihilist who loathes life when I cannot resign myself to the one I'm handed and which is a piece of crap;

behaving badly when I simply refuse to wear a servant's livery and all its accessories;

demonstrating, lastly, an unacceptable pessimism— there, I've said the word, when it's my frustrated taste for beauty, grandeur, and grace that drives me to sorrow, then from sorrow to anger, and from anger to conversation where I rediscover, gently, a certain jocular enthusiasm.

For the seventh condition, which is

The principle of equality,

I heartily recommend, ladies and gentlemen, that you consider the behavior of animals, whose habits when greeting one another are often prodigiously instructive to humans.

Examine two canines of different kinds. They meet. And observe each other. And inevitably draw closer. Do they attach, as do their masters, any importance to the exterior signs of their social backgrounds? Not in the least. Which immediately allows them to establish a relationship that is cordial, warm, even frenetic.

Now take Monsieur C., psychologist, with a monthly salary of fifteen thousand francs. Place him before a poor man whose total income is twice nothing. Study closely the reactions of both men: Monsieur C. seems the more ill-at-ease. Since he is a man of modern ideals, he is not going to fall into the trap of charity, which is nothing more, he has read, than the flip side of a bad conscience. Believing, quite philosophically, that charity serves only to absolve the guilt of the well-to-do in order to perpetuate the misery of the miserable, he renounces charity. Sublimely. What, then, will he undertake so as to remain faithful to his ideals? Will he speak to this needy man? Share his own meal with him? His ideas? Suggest a bit of fornication? No, our philanthropist will offer this unfortunate, guess what, a pamphlet. From this insurmountable misunderstanding comes catastrophic consequences. The poor man, naturally, is not pleased with Monsieur C.'s attitude and tells him so in colorful terms. Whence this bitter axiom uttered by wicked souls:

—

The poor have no morality.

—

Amended by this much more appealing one:

—

The bourgeois used to have their poor.
Now it's the intellectuals who have theirs.

—

That, it seems, is called progress. By the way, we must hope that no government will deprive the intellectuals of their poor. Because by soaking up their spare time (and you know intellectuals have plenty of that), the poor prevent these thinkers from doing harm elsewhere.

But let's get back to our subject, which is equality. As you have gathered, ladies, gentlemen, and kiddies, having repeatedly asserted his pre-eminence over the canines, man could never lower himself by proving their inferior in matters of social justice. Hence this decisive aphorism we trumpet before you to dispel your nagging doubts.

—

Every man who converses places his interlocutor
on an equal footing with himself.

—

And this second maxim that completes the above and is on every point in harmony with the Gospel:

—

All souls are equal, all are entitled to converse.

—

Rich or poor, rascal or angel, scholar or ignoramus, Flemish or Walloon—all men, my dear children, for it is to your pure hearts that I speak, all men are worthy of conversing in their own language within their culture and form of government.

Rumor hath it that Monsieur Tribulet, although a professed Catholic, thinks absolutely otherwise. We might have known. But let's not be as demagogic as Monsieur Tribulet is obtuse. And make no mistake: we certainly do not intend either to deny the real distinctions between a man who plays the stock market and a man who pushes a broom, thereby simply perpetuating their class differences—or to exaggerate the importance of said differences, thus turning these people into caricatures.

But what then? Then we must—even knowing that the distance between us and our neighbor can be more impassable than the greatest ocean, such is the power of prejudice—we must agree to reconnoiter the other person's territory, to discover overlooked relationships between what was falsely separated, to perform grafts, to mix and match, to invent other wacko languages, to fuck lowlifes and bring forth the mutants of the third millennium, I'm getting carried away, and in another second, I'd even believe it all myself.

Example.

You observe a guy from a housing project. He speaks a French far removed from the literary kind. Wears Nikes and a baseball cap. And lives in the maze of the projects almost like a cockroach.

A denizen of the projects examines you in turn and thinks, This man studying me, who doesn't know how to dance or sing or trash enemy objects, like cars and so on, is he human?

That is the first reaction of two individuals who belong—in spite of appearances—to the same species. And we speak of our "fellow" men! I have to laugh. But let's not be negative. We'll get complaints.

Then these two individuals meet, and the impossible business between them can begin. Always the same aporia! But it helps me to keep saying this. You think I'm contradicting myself, don't you! That I'm piously preaching about reaching out to one another, only to claim in the next breath that it's impossible! And even if it were, should we give up trying? Look at Don Quixote and Sancho Panza, Toby and Trim (my little favorites), Ahab and his whale, Lucienne (it's the word "whale" that brings her to mind because Lulu, my Lulu, was in several ways rather like a whale, don't misunderstand me, I'm not being the slightest bit sarcastic, a whale, my Lulu, who spent most of her time beached on the bed, belly up, emitting marine odors I found utterly intoxicating), where was I? Ahab and his whale. Lucienne and I. Sublime couples. Impossible couples. Forever divine.

But let's get back for a moment to that idea of equality which has been dishonored by so much abuse and empty gargling. In conversation, may I remind you, the participants are equals, in the noble sense of the word. Not a problem, you'll say, in the land of the Rights of Man. Of course. If you exclude those whose words head inevitably toward the bottom of the barrel, I'm thinking in particular—no offense meant—of my former department head, Monsieur Martres, and of the teachers I knew who were so full of themselves, and the catechizers, fault-find-ers, pedants, high priests, viragos of all ages and sorts, divers druids, the hermeneutists and their ilk, I must be forgetting some, the bankers whose entry into the paradise of conversation remains problematic, despite their sizable fortunes (credit cards, take note, are not always accepted). And if these folks are disqualified, well that's too bad, tough shit, they're a royal pain in the ass, those creeps.

Excuse me, I'm out of bounds. For a lecturer of my stature, that's really fucking up. Which is to be avoided at all costs in a conversation that particularly requires, admire my feel for transitions,

A sense of proportion: The eighth condition.

What is a sense of proportion? Can you tell me, ladies and gentlemen? A sense of proportion is nothing else but prudence in the expression of one's thoughts, especially when they're intent on trouble.

Although I'm more than convinced that none of you is plotting sedition against a government as competent and excellent as ours, I would like, as a precaution, to present you with this set of axioms:

—

Do not flaunt the fact that you are a rebel. Advance your boldest ideas as if they were mere trifles. And claim credit for them twenty years later, when they have become common parlance.

—

Spare us any pomposity. It's the echo of an empty head. And if you have nothing to say, you can always keep quiet. It's amazing how few people think of that!

—

Do not harp loudly on your convictions, for you will seem unsure of them yourself. When my Lucienne, for example, used to shout, We should eat to live and not live to eat, my beloved obviously had her doubts about that. And was shouting to convince herself.

—

To avoid growing old before your time, it is vital to remain calm in the face of bullshit. Look at me. Don't I seem young and sprightly?

—

Standing before a painting by Bacon, do not exclaim, How beautiful, how beautiful. Bellowing about beauty is not, as you believe, poetic. It's just utterly grotesque.

—

Do not laugh at your own jokes, *please*. Do you want to seem like a fat Bavarian tourist in Majorca? I can already tell from your furrowed brows: you're wondering if Lucienne was from Bavaria . . . If you'd been paying attention, you would know she was born in Spain. In Fatarella. Province of Tarragona. April 12, 1940. Died January 2, 1999. She just missed out on the third millennium celebrations. Rotten luck, poor thing. And she was so fond of official festivities!

—

Do not tear your hair out over your misfortunes. That makes people laugh. Which isn't at all what you want. Do I, a widower for barely two months, indulge in such shenanigans? Do I bewail my fate? Break down in tears?

—

If someone bothers you, don't splutter, don't lash out, don't pitch a fit. Stay icy calm. And let the dogs bark. They usually wind up fighting among themselves.

—

In all things, including the most vile, keep a sense of proportion. Don't waste any effort, which is both tiring and futile. Save your energy, I pray you, for other occasions there is no need to mention.

—

And learn to temper your indignation. It is often merely the bitter poison of your uneasy conscience. If you must, obtain a prescription for a mild tranquilizer or soothe your seething feelings with a cold shower.

—

Does that mean one must keep silent and grovel abjectly, you'll ask me.

No, a thousand times no. The essential thing is to say it with flowers, I mean subtly, and politely: Oh after you, please do, you're so welcome. Suggest, for example, that this world is fantastic provided you're born into it with a silver spoon in your mouth. That the fascinating idea that we live to consume-consume-consume all the way to the tomb might warrant, perhaps, just the teensiest second thought. That the present economic order touted as inevitable has its merits, of course, but couldn't possibly be perfect—all the above proffered with silly smiles, the usual twittering song and dance. And that by getting our butts—I mean tongues—in gear it might be possible to gear up against misfortune and deflect its terrible trajectory. It's feasible. We have the means. We have the means, good Lord! We just need to use them better. No, after all, don't say that. Pose instead as a thinker who couldn't care less about action. It's more chic.

You wish to assure yourselves, ladies and gentlemen, that you are endowed with that sense of proportion I have been extolling to you with disproportionate enthusiasm, very funny. It's quite simple. Present yourself before a crowd. You hear roars of laughter? Then you are completely bereft of the desired quality and have made distressing concessions to the common taste: labored platitudes, sentimental drivel, and knowing winks. You have failed. Ciao.

Applied to writing, a sense of proportion necessarily requires the elimination of empty phrases, clichés, affectations, and guff. Then certain books might collapse like empty bags, you'll say. But let the writers in question take heart. The reading public of Cintegabelle, like its international counterpart, delights in empty bags, as long as they are perfectly harmless. I haven't waited sixty years to start mincing words now! Yikes!

This sense of proportion in no way excludes, I need hardly add, either vivacity, or incisiveness, or fire, or brimstone, or madness, or fury, or giddiness. It is the inner conflict that leads me to choose respect, only to long more ardently for disrespect. The vacillation that makes me hesitate constantly between my lightness of touch (a rhetorical politeness, actually) and my seriousness of purpose (springing from a radical insolence of thought), I'm not at all certain about what I'm telling you and am

simply repeating what I've read in books, as all lectur-
ers do, it pads things out. Let's carry on with our lofty
language—something will surely come of it. The sense of
proportion, I was saying, is that narrow, winding path
between two chasms where reason skirts madness, where
ascesis corrects excess, where irony mocks sorrow, where
the sense of proportion keeps a constant rein on dispro-
portion. Whence, ladies and gentlemen, this luminous
aphorism:

—

Conversation is an art for tightrope walkers.

—

That such tightrope walkers broke their backs a long
time ago, we know. Because ever since Monsieur Tribulet
and his kind have become powerful, the sense of proportion has been watered down to a taste for the average, by
which I mean mediocrity. In fact Tribulet and his tribe
have this in common: they mistake dullness for discretion, hypocrisy for courtesy, constipation for restraint.
They feel they must repress the dreams that haunt them,
must make discourse less prickly, less tart and crude,

more flat, more toothless, what can I say, just plain dead, leaving only what is acceptable and decent. In other words, nothing.

But who is this Tribulet I've been dinning, since the beginning, into your ears? And what the hell is he doing here? Monsieur Tribulet has provided a most pertinent image of himself, which he has hung on the gate of his house: BEWARE OF DOG. A harsh judgment indeed, but Monsieur Tribulet shows considerable perspicacity. One must be wary of him, for he has that sad and wicked habit of projecting onto others the unfairness of his own life. He has the servile soul of a dog, barks at every passing stranger, enjoys groveling, and is a natural-born bootlicker. Monsieur Tribulet makes no bones about it: those unfamiliar hands poised to pet his thin coat—he'd like to see them turned into dog food! If only it were up to him! But unlike his own dog, Monsieur Tribulet has learned to hoard his petty resentments, keeping them hidden, coddled, nourished on a small helping of daily hatred, until the long-awaited day when a master will yell at him: Attack!

We have now arrived, ladies and gentlemen, at the ninth condition for conversation, which is

An insouciant disregard for time.

We were just speaking to you about Monsieur Tribulet. Jacques Balin, our local mover-and-shaker, naturally despises Monsieur Tribulet's distrustful nature, his dreadful bitterness, his blatant lack of curiosity, and that taste for the average he abjectly mistakes for a sense of proportion. Not for anything in this world would Jacques Balin wish to resemble Monsieur Tribulet—for whom we feel a sudden compassion. The human soul is fickle indeed!

As for Jacques Balin, moderation is not for him. Thinking fast and furiously, talking fast and furiously, ruining others in a trice and getting rich the same way, that's his ideal. If he's ever at a loss for a few moments, he panics: is he losing his grip? But he quickly forgets that grim hypothesis. And immediately cooks up another one just as foolish. Before going off to play squash. Squash is tops.

Balin, you will have realized, is a man in a hurry. His feelings have to climax fast. His thoughts have to spit out results. And he's quick to call slow-witted anyone who takes the time to think something through, to reason and reply with due deliberation.

Because Balin wants to know it all and right now, have an answer for everything when he understands nothing, and wrap up projects as swiftly and profitably as possible. No relief for this man. No vacation for his mind. Is there one chance in a million that some day this fellow will fling himself across his mahogany desk and wonder: What the fuck am I doing with my life? Why so much speed, so much zeal?

We have good reason to doubt it. Monsieur Balin will stay as he is. A gentleman held in high esteem, with an opinion on everything but a knowledge of nothing. He will be, in short, unfit for conversation. As he is for life.

He in no way resembles the man of conversation, who couldn't care less, you see, about time, or anything else. The conversational man makes his way at a stroll, dawdling, digressing, and sometimes, like donkeys, going backwards. An occasional swerve, a swift kick, an impetuous leap, a thoughtful pause. Then a sudden about-face. But a slow pace, always, when moving along. For he knows that from slowness can come illumination. And he loves illumination as much as slowness.

Essentially, conversation presupposes—and here we come to a canonical axiom that challenges, I won't hesitate to say, the global economic system:

—

Conversation presupposes a perfect disregard for time.

—

In other words, ladies and gentlemen, it implies free time, time that is literally free, liberated from the meanness of work, of chores and toil, just as Petronius dreamed of in the *Satyricon,* time enough to enjoy the chirping of sparrows, the lament of the wind tormenting birch trees, the color of the sky before it clouds over, and other pastoral themes that are dear to my heart, in spite of what I say, time to talk about arts and pleasures, time for oneself and time for others, time to potter around, eudaemonic time, dear hearts, time to "find yourself," says Marie-Jo, who cuts my hair and has none of this time, in her life set in curlers for a permanent-death. In short, my friends, an artist's time. My Lulu's time.

My Lulu performed her principle operations without worrying for a moment about watches, alarm clocks, chronometers, and other instruments of time-torture. I'm talking about her alimentary operations (she ruminated, in fact, much more than she ate), her locomotive operations (her traveling speed along her main track, linking the bed to the refrigerator, was about ten yards an hour, for Lucienne advanced with her legs wide apart so as not to irritate the chafed and inflamed skin of her inner thighs), and her mental operations, at which she broke, I must say, all records for indolence, since Lucienne was a very private person who meditated at length before vouchsafing any reply.

Wha? she would finally shout, when I quizzed her on some chapter of our life. Dear girl! One would have thought, stupidly, that she was paying no attention to me, absorbed as she was in her TV soap operas, for

Lucienne had a very contemplative nature. But not at all—my Lucienne was simply taking the time to mull over a thought in all its aspects to reduce it to its hard core: Whence and what is it? A kind of short version of the Socratic method. The first canon of the *Critique* according to Emmanuel Kant. Whence and what is it? The reduction of our perplexity before the mayhem of meaning to a clear and easy-to-remember concept. Wha? screamed at my unwilling ears so that I would finally get the idea.

But who then, ladies and gentlemen, outside of a few veterans and pensioners, lucky invalids, or widowers like me, who then has this kind of free and unshackled time? Who among us can live and prosper off the life of his soul? Must men go so far as to promote the demise of their spouses to get their hands on their wives' pensions? That's black humor. In poor taste. Please excuse me. If I'm joking around, it's to counteract my distress. To distress my distress, if I may say so. Until it drops dead. That's my method. It's as good as any others. Which are more costly. How do we attain this ideal time, I was saying, that the ancients called *otium*? Should our government, in defiance of its economy, allow everyone to be unemployed? Capital questions, and I leave them in your hands. Because you ought to have a few things on your hands to discuss. As for me, I will now continue with that previously established Classification from which we have, in my opinion, too often digressed.

According to the temporal criteria we have just defined, we find ourselves forced to eject from conversation, in descending order, ranging from the great Captains of Industry down to the smallest retailers and secondhand dealers, all persons who, by devoting themselves exclusively to stealing other people's money, pride themselves on not having a minute to spare for conversation. Which is the very definition, according to Epictetus, of the common man. A brief quotation, now and again, can't hurt. True or false, it doesn't matter. But from antiquity, if possible. Now back to our thieves. These unfortunates, we feel, are on the wrong track, having missed the point. Because conversation is not incompatible with theft. Conversation, ladies and gentlemen, is theft, a subject we will address later. Unless something else crops up.

One more detail: in our Cintegabellian population, which does not have a strong sense of social justice (unlike the Bordètes, for example, one of Henri Michaux's imaginary tribes), the aforementioned persons, who make their fortunes at the expense of others, are not often accused of crimes and only rarely condemned to death. This explains their excessive numbers. Must we enact more drastic laws against them? That is a step, my dear friends, we currently hesitate to take. We will perhaps be kind enough to analyze the ins and outs of this crucial question in a forthcoming treatise. If the demands of fame, that is, leave us enough time. Which I doubt. For the moment, let us attack, if I may put it that way, the last condition. Which we should inscribe in letters of gold. For it is the sine qua non of conversation. I am referring to:

Freedom.

Please take note, if you will:

—

Conversation is a bindweed.

—

Conversation is a rumba.

—

Conversation is an insomniac.
It keeps speech awake.

—

Conversation is a grass that grows
between paving stones, to separate them.

—

Conversation is by turns acid, adorable, African, ad-
dicted to shadows, bizarre, bushy, bold, coy as a woman,
bantering, cunning, combative, comical, contradictory,
devoted to surprises, devil-may-care, digestive, digressive,
doesn't do today what it can do tomorrow, it's disruptive,
eccentric, erotic, explosive, enthusiastic and tickled by
its own enthusiasm, feverish, flowing, feminine, frisky,
ferrets constantly through the idea shop, is fond of games
and gambling, a gourmand, as good-for-nothing as a
dream, independent, impetuous, inopportune, jaunty,
kinky, languid, lascivious, mocking, mordant, mysteri-

ous, nocturnal, never takes anything for granted, is open, piquant, proceeds by leaps and bounds, rambles, runs the gamut, is riotous, as staunch and sad as the truth, saucy, sometimes as salty as the sea, swift to set sail for anywhere (how could you catch up?), tender, undulating, vibrant, whispery, and zingy—that's conversation!

It's everything and nothing! I hear the sticklers object with one voice.

Poor fools who have no idea that it is precisely when speeches are polished to death, conventional, and all of a piece, when their rhetoric is unchanging and worn ragged, when the conviction that drives them is as unshakable as a wall—it's when these speeches, as I was saying, are set, rectilinear, aware of their conclusions from their very beginnings, that they have every likelihood of saying just any old thing.

Conversation, ladies and gentlemen, conversation, real conversation, the one we love and defend body and soul, is like thought, as fragile, as mobile as thought, and equally infinite in its masks and its cheap finery: in a word, free. A pretty pronouncement, don't you think?

But how does it translate into reality?—a chief concern of my Lucienne, who, despite her limited understanding, displayed outstanding disputative powers. What are you yakking about? she would cry in response to my philosophical speculations, banishing pointless questions to their absurdity so that the pith of the matter stood revealed. What are you jabbering? This, my Lulu. That free conversation makes free with current opinions as well as time-honored dogmas. Even better, that it pisses on them, with our blithe approval. Because

—

conversation does not follow the herd.

—

It likes to go off on its own. Off on tangents. Walking in the fresh air. And poking around where it shouldn't.

Nevertheless, conversation knows that there is no such thing as pure freedom, or judgment devoid of bias. It knows that prejudices are our lot and our misfortune, and that no one escapes the effects of what is called Communication. But instead of subjecting itself to these impediments or rejecting them outright, conversation uses them, toys with them. Patiently, it transfigures them. It makes art from them. As soon as I get to the theoretical part, I get all worked up, carried away. It's just that I was deprived of this for so long. By my lambkin. It scared her. Poor thing, it was pitiful. Her fear made her blurt out harsh words. It's the same with all the frightened souls of this earth. Will you shut up or what, she'd yell at me, pummeling me on the back whenever I tried to lead her through the twists and turns of abstract thought. Shut your trap, she'd scream at me, until I gave up and said I was sorry. So sorry, in fact, that I stopped sharing my transcendental cogitation with her. So as not to scare her anymore, my shrinking violet. Then I stopped talking to her at all. It was simpler. We only spoke when truly necessary. Remarks like, I'm beat, I'm starving, or interjections such as, You've got fucking nerve. In short, we were approaching the subliminal. As in modern novels.

But today I can return to the sensual delights of pure knowledge without fear of terrorizing my Lulu. I am in the process, moreover, of putting together an exceptional library, I say this without any false modesty. In two months, I have purchased at the Ombres Blanches bookstore at least three hundred works. Thanks to the small legacy I inherited and the comfy pension that now comes to me. A widower's life has some consolations, let's face it. Where were we?

You have understood, ladies and gentlemen: the man of conversation is the artist, the lively mind, the loner, the one who follows no master, bows down before nothing, and seeks authority for his discourse only in himself. He is free, fraternal, forgiving, not in the least stingy—what else?—has wit enough and to spare, loves beauty, is quite likeable, and so on. The man of conversation, in short, is me. I cannot conceal it from you any longer.

How do I do it? I recycle. That's my secret. Now you know. I select an opinion here, in Monsieur Tribulet's butcher shop; intercept another one there, in the newspaper; filch an idea from Seneca, mull over a sentence from Saint-Simon, then examine my harvest, assemble the components, shuffle them, rearrange them until they are mine, until they come to life. And then no one in the world can challenge my ownership. I am master and man to my thoughts.

But ever since the death of great ideas (may they rest in peace), ever since self-interest has reigned supreme and unchallenged by most people, who dread seeming passé, humanity has been in danger of having nothing solid to rely on, of believing that all things are equal, justice and injustice, the grain and its chaff, in short, of saying the hell with it, let's just flip a coin.

We wise men, however, we deep thinkers, we brace ourselves against a few stable points. We love truth and we love liberty. Which are not, good grief, empty words, how can I put this? They are our bow and arrow, our thirst and wellspring, I shout this, I proclaim it, at the risk of being taken for a madman or condemned by those who kneel in silence and abandon their desire for truth and freedom. Which we love, I insist, which we sometimes approach, but never pluck, for like flowers, once picked, they wither and die, so we seek them constantly, we seek them eternally, without ever reaching them, except in infinity. Hence, ladies and gentlemen, this unbeatable axiom:

—

Conversation doesn't wear out.

—

That's another of its qualities considered dangerous to the global marketplace, which seems to bank on the deterioration of things, including language.

Let's say this again, at the risk of seeming heavy-handed: the man of conversation relies on a logic that dispenses with all finality, save that of partaking freely and joyously in the search for rational truth. No schemes. No tricks. No sleazy gimmicks for this person who doesn't want to win, or lose, or persuade, or dissuade, or judge, or condemn, or flatter, or attack, or accuse, or protest, or proselytize, or put a good face on things, or win the world over to his side, or succeed, or fail, still less sell himself, or get rich. Because

—

conversation is a nonprofit organization.

—

Thank God, I have my widower's pension, as I just told you. But I like to repeat pleasant things. A tidy sum, no complaints there. Somewhat depleted by the funeral expenses. Much heavier than I would ever have expected. I decided to go first class. Solid oak, satin lining, ornate handles. A huge floral arrangement. I went all out. Didn't want any criticism from the psychiatrist brother-in-law. That asshole. By spending lavishly, I took the wind out of his sails. All that constant analytic hot air. Even though I consider those expenditures money thrown away. Worm food.

A lovely little nest egg that will at last allow me to devote myself to the affairs of the mind. Which my Lulu forbade me to do, fearing, poor love, that my health would suffer, along with her purse. But then she passed on before I did! Death is unfair. And now I'm the one who controls her purse-strings. That changes your perspective. Amazing how it changes your perspective!

To recapitulate:

The man of conversation, ladies, gentlemen, and demoiselles, owes it to himself to sit in the company of his interlocutor—with his rear end softly cushioned, his mind open to both the beauty and ugliness of things, at perfect liberty in his time and his thoughts—and cherish the truth.

Since no administration has determined the precise number of persons capable of fulfilling said parameters, we have compensated for this serious oversight by tallying up those inhabitants of Cintegabelle who are fit for conversation.

After eliminating chatterboxes, patterboxes, loudmouths, soliloquists, and other cacophonists, we have established that only forty-eight people are suited to the art of conversation: forty-two of them are reasonably adept, five are talented, one is a genius, and guess who that is.

What must we, from these blunt statistics, infer?

That conversation, my dear friends, is an anomaly, an aberration, a deviation. That conversation is a miracle. And that those most suited to it are rare, scattered far and wide, misunderstood, harassed, exposed to dark forces. It seems hopeless. However . . .

. . . even if only two of them were to show up, ladies and gentlemen, for some conversation at eleven o'clock of an evening at the Café des Ormes, which has become our fief, I say this for anyone who would like to join us, the more the merrier, even if only two were to appear we would be saved. For verily I say unto you,

—

conversation is a fire that can spread
and set the whole world aflame.

—

Sometimes I think I'm Jesus. I have his charisma, obviously. And Lulu is Mary Magdalene. Only chubbier. And less distraught. I have the charisma of Jesus, but I lack his good looks. Can you imagine him with big ears and a cowlick? Shown like that in Giotto's frescoes? Can't you just see that?

What? What is it? Suddenly I see a skeptical look on your faces, it's rather unsettling. Exactly what is the problem? You think the numbers I gave you are too pessimistic, that there are more Cintegabellois who know how to converse than I just said, that you yourselves, moreover, that Féfé, a man-about-town of your acquaintance . . . Society people, let's talk about them! That will help us further refine our definition of the man of conversation. Of whom the socialite is merely the counterfeit.

A case in point.

Take Féfé, born in Paris, the son of a nobody, a perfect whore. Féfé says he's wasting away in this hole, Cintegabelle, and he spends most of his time in Toulouse, the regional capital. Where he is everywhere at once. At the K7 Cinéma, at the Grand Café de l'Opéra, at the Galerie Meurisse, at the Capoul . . . Because although the man of conversation is fond of intimate circles, Féfé is intoxicated by crowds. There is no party he doesn't attend, no discussion where he doesn't spout nonsense. Féfé hops from one mob to another. Tosses off a compliment here. Launches some slander there. Doesn't listen to a thing. Waxes indignant over the latest injustice. Gobbles up the macrobiotic diet of an actress who's into mysticism. Raves about a certain film. Pooh-poohs it in the next breath. Wears himself

out with witticisms. Makes jibes that fall flat. Sings dithy-
rambs or drips with disdain, depending on which way the
wind is blowing. It appears from these activities that

—

social success demands the athletic skills of an acrobat,

—

skills of which Féfé is justly proud. But Féfé tires
easily. All that simpering, that fluttering, those dreary
old catty remarks, that backbiting larded with fulsome
praise, all that posturing, really, it's exhausting. Féfé goes
home wiped out, snaps back at his wife—an unfortunate
woman named Nathalie—and sometimes says Shit, fuck
off, leave me the hell alone, then bemoans his life to induce
her to forgive him. My life, he says, is one of constant
dissipation. I'm sick, he says, of phoniness. Overworked,
battered by so many pointless stunts, my intelligence, he
says, is going to seed. Forced to hobnob endlessly with
halfwits and scatterbrains, he says, I find the world vile.
Talking without having anything to say, he says, lavishing insincere compliments, it's just backbreaking.

—

Life in fashionable society is one long martyrdom.

—

The next day, however, Féfé sets out once more on his painful pilgrimage with amazing devotion. Expected to know and judge everything, he surfs the surface of things, sometimes barely grazing them with the grace of a sylph.

Like a hairdresser whose duties require him to make small talk without getting too nosy, Féfé discusses everything but shuns anything important. Why? Because Féfé is a runaway. Féfé is running from who knows what that clearly terrifies him. If Féfé sparkles for all he's worth, wears himself out in pirouettes, and pours such energy into bon mots, it's only in the constant hope of escaping the terror driving him doggedly to be everywhere at once. Féfé, ladies and gentlemen, is running away from himself. Féfé, at top speed, joins the fleeing horde of those fleeing themselves. Whereas the man of conversation, a modern Diogenes, sets out boldly to meet someone else so that together they may think and talk about the enigma that is man.

What windy, murky, flowery language!

Perhaps, my friends. But to say that the decline of conversation is linked to the decline of France is not just bombast. May I remind amnesiacs that Rome in its day experienced a similar collapse and never recovered. But enough of that! Far be it from us to lament the loss of splendors past. And if conversation today has lost some of its luster, let us wager that tomorrow it will gain in—it will gain in what? Now I am assailed by doubts, trembling at the thought that future generations will have forgotten even its name.

I was born midway through a century in which one spoke of love, when conversing was a pleasure, an art, a necessity. Could I endure a world in which conversation would be thrown away, or worse, reduced to nothing? And can I resign myself to dying without the hope that conversation will survive? But here I am giving in to melancholic feelings. That's not nice. And it's time for me to perk up again. Because now I must deal with the objections of the last holdouts.

As a matter of fact, a few timid souls in our little town claim that conversation is not only a crummy old thing best left to senior citizens (thanks a lot!), but a dangerously outmoded idea that refuses in the most brazen way to obey the so-called laws of the marketplace. Because conversation is, let's sum it up, free, useless, delightful, uncontrollable, in no way profitable, not tied down by anything, and doesn't wear out—in other words, twice as dangerous as sex, therefore doubly to be censured.

And if you reply to these petty people, as did in bygone days the Marquise, our cousin, I'm joking, that conversation is after all but a seed, a tiny insignificant seed lost in the vastness of the world, they will object, most indignantly, that this particular seed doesn't play fair (meaning what?—that it won't let itself be ground into flour, fine!) and that by slipping through the meshes of the system, it risks throwing the machines of time and commerce out of whack, starting a chain reaction of disorder from Cintegabelle to Tokyo, with panic in the stock markets, the collapse of the dollar, and so on to the final crash.

These objections, my dear friends, seem a bit exaggerated. Not to mention ridiculous. After investigation, we have established that they originated with a few persons in the world of finance whose judgment is contaminated, it appears, by the deplorable mania of spending every single second doing mental arithmetic.

Nevertheless, we would like to reassure these people: we have no intention of harming a system that has produced and continues to produce such wonderful results. There are only two billion starving souls in the world, and almost as many illiterates. In other words, no big deal. But if, in the end, these financial wizards were to feel somewhat threatened by conversation, we still wouldn't give in, and with all due respect, we'd tell them to go screw themselves. And as far away as possible.

We now feel peppy enough, ladies and gentlemen, to tackle . . .

Part Three of our lecture,

which will be devoted to a few examples of conversation.

Since there are as many kinds of conversation, ladies and gentlemen, as there are of women, it would be folly to try listing them all. We shall confine ourselves, therefore, to only five of the most familiar kinds: amorous conversation, literary conversation, political conversation, patriotic conversation, and conversation with the dead.

So, first of all,

Amorous Conversation.

I see you starting to squirm. You're burning with impatience. One might think you came only to hear me talk about love. Well, ladies and gentlemen, that simply proves this: you are definitely French.

Because France, ladies and gentlemen, is the incomparable land of the love of love. Because France is the land where love is spoken before it is made. Because France is the land of amorous preambles. We preamble in France. We preamble ad infinitum. We preamble, we ramble. From dawn to dusk. We introduce love with prefatory remarks, we give off sparks, but we leave it at that. The first delicate kiss has barely landed when the flag goes up: all done. Which is very irritating. And has led a few mean-spirited people to stipulate that

—

an eloquent talker is an impotent lover.

—

An axiom I contest most vigorously, I who have been addressing you for almost an hour, but an axiom that has led me to examine this sexual weakness that some call impotence and that supposedly even forms part of our national character.

But first, if you'll allow me, a short historical overview.

No matter how far back you go in our archives, nowhere in France will you find a reference work for the strictly amorous domain in question. No *Kama Sutra* to instruct us. No encyclopedic compilation of the 236 erotic positions and their 418 variations. No treatise on amorous strategy, such as the Chinese have, presenting the 36 ways of attacking a fortress as well as the 28 ruses for targeting its weak spots and taking matters, so to speak, in hand. Nothing even remotely similar.

This major deficiency, which might well have mortified, weakened, and subdued an entire people, proved to be one of our greatest strengths.

To compensate for this lack, the French came up with the idea of conversing.

They taught their tongues the way one trains an animal.

And instead of making love, they decided to say it.

A masterstroke! Sublime turnabout! The French were for a long time excused from those fornicatory practices that diminish intellective abilities and drive human beings into appalling outbursts.

The French invented love, *le grand amour,* the only one worthwhile: the love that announces and serenades itself. And being in love, that amorous state universally considered a moment of temporary insanity here below, gave the wings of angels to conversation in France.

That's when the French ran into this most painful and delightful dilemma: in substituting for sex, conversation did not, however, scratch its itch, which wasn't the least of its paradoxes. Worse, it made the itch worse. Inflamed it. Brought it to incandescence. In a way, conversation lit a fire up your ass, I'm using your words, my Lucienne, to bring you just a little back to life. The conclusion was unavoidable:

—

the aphrodisiac of conversation is a danger to morality.

—

After a few hours of babble, in fact, the French could seek relief from their satyriasis only by applying astringent lotions, turning to ejaculatory prayers, reading works in verse, or fomenting a few revolutions. Which they did. With the success that we know.

Some hot-blooded diehards, however, on whom those anti-pruritic potions had no effect, secretly indulged in a bit of fellation. Others turned to fornication, usually reserved for animals, foreigners, and illiterates. Once those expedients had been disposed of, though, conversation sprang up again, friskier than ever, more subtle, more far-reaching, forgetting its purpose, heading for the heights, climbing into the clouds. A blessed era!

Were there particular subjects recommended for these adorable chats? One theme predominated: the Other. The Other's lips. The Other's eyes. The Other's Mind. The Other's goodness. Never her ass. Go figure. Then once more from the top. The Other's lips. The Other's eyes . . . and around the track again. A hundred times, the same quivering steps along the same paths. Relentlessly.

Did you fear becoming boring? When pigs fly! Women were so constructed that they never tired of hearing the exegeses they inspired.

Were you starting to lose interest? Was toiling at your love life turning into a chore? You drooped with fatigue while reciting your stanzas? It was because you weren't in love anymore! Then you would shift, imperceptibly, from amorous conversation to artistic conversation. And if you were an utter cad, you would definitely steer your companion toward political conversation, the perfect antidote to love, as we'll see later on.

With Lucienne, however, the first time, things diverged a bit from this scenario. The preamble was reduced to the bare minimum. The business completed lickety-split. The disappointment huge, I must confess.

Given our complete lack of experience and the difference in our weight, getting connected turned out to be quite difficult. The ascent, first of all, was arduous. I lost my grip several times, always caught by her magnificent arms. Arriving on the central plateau, I clung there askew for a while until I succeeded in bracing myself, with my feet parked against her knees. As for the coupling itself, we had to try several approaches. She below and myself on top. Perforce. Considering our respective volumes. First, pointing in the same direction. Then head to toe. Sheer horror in the scenery department. And back in the same direction again. Discretion prevents me from saying any more.

But our haste was fatal to the little chat we'd begun ten minutes earlier. And we never managed, throughout our life together, to get back to it. In fact we wrote it off. We even lost the hang of it altogether. That was our tragedy. Looking high and low for other ways to connect with one another. Despairing of ever finding any that could satisfy us. Like Dante's poor damned souls. Which we were. Without realizing it. And so damned twice over. Because the both of us suffered hellishly over that gaping absence of loving words that nothing else could fill. Nothing. Not even the sexual jousts in which we made, as we grew older, extraordinary progress. In the department of sobriety, first of all. But especially in the area of speed. A few minutes, at the end, were enough to calm our ardor. I'm speaking of the period before the disaster. When Lucienne was in her prime. And I find myself dreaming about the performances we would have put on if my Lulu, my exquisite one, had remained operational.

So when she died, at the end of a life cruelly deprived of verbal pleasures—but is a life without such pleasures still a life?—I vowed to devote my best efforts to the renewal (that word offends my delicate ears), to the Defense and Illustration of Conversation and to the return to fashionable favor of the Epithalamium. Madame Flippe raises a hand? Madame Flippe would like to know what an Epithalamium is? It is a nuptial poem, my dear lady. A lost tradition. Alas, alas.

Yet as I advanced in my struggle, as my dossier swelled, as I accumulated inquiries, I became convinced that my Lucienne and I were not isolated cases at all, as I had long believed. Conversation was growing rare, that was an undeniable fact, in Cintegabelle as in the whole of France. Conversation was getting the hell out. In a death agony. Brain dead. Without anyone coming to the rescue.

Except me. The only one. The minstrel of Cintegabelle.

And even though it wasn't like me to long for the good old days—the good old days, frankly, I didn't give a flaming fuck about them, I'd even go so far as to say they gave me the creeps, the good old days, everything that's old, in fact, gives me the creeps—I was sometimes, I was saying, seized with a feeling of nostalgia. Was conversation going to carry off into its grave the love with which it was, in a way, consubstantial? I wiped away a tear at that gloomy prospect, and with a dreadful pang in my heart, I penned this dramatic axiom:

—

The end of conversation tolls the knell for love.

—

But I cannot believe it, my friends. I do not believe it. What I just said was meant as a kind of exorcism. I simply don't know anymore. And would rather change the subject before I sink into endless sorrow.

And since we certainly have need of consolation, I suggest that you now turn your attention to a much less painful subject, namely,

Literary Conversation.

Literary conversation also possesses this above-mentioned virtue: it may pleasantly take the place of sexual matters. It may even cool them off. Freeze them solid. Thus proving quite useful in our relational life, as my psychiatrist brother-in-law says, in that eucharistic tone of his I loathe.

Before I define and analyze literary conversation, a few words about the circumstances in which I had to employ it.

As I told you a while ago, I went off to Paris some time in December, abandoning my poor lamb, who was already ill, with the intention of offering to publishers the manuscript of this lecture I'm lavishing on you. I was accompanied by my friend, the local writer who is an expert on crafts. For the two of us, Paris would be a movable feast.

Through a series of accidents it would be tedious to recount, we managed, during our visit, to attend a literary cocktail party held in a vast apartment on the posh

Avenue Marceau. Here is what I observed there. Which made a deep impression on me.

While small deals in commercial literature were being made and unmade off in various corners, I watched two large circles form. Curious, I approached one of them, a group surrounding a red-faced and self-important man who expounded on his work with visible enthusiasm, while around him gravitated individuals whose broad smiles and batting eyelids showed they shared his admiration. I elbowed my way into their company unnoticed, since they were busy clapping, laughing at the poet's jokes, bowing and scraping, fawning and sighing. Still, I'm relieved to say, they did refrain from fondling him.

Intrigued by such devotion, I briefly questioned my neighbor to the right, who simply stared at me as if I'd been a bag of plaster. I tried again with someone else. Who gave me the cold shoulder. Disappointed, I turned to a third guest. Who replied with a nasty remark, mistaking malice for wit.

A literary cocktail party is an ugly thing,

—

I decided. But I wished to understand the reason for
such foul moods. I was already thinking about the detailed
report I would give my Lucienne (a touch embellished re-
garding myself, barely exaggerated as to the rest). Simply
to amuse her. I loved to amuse her. I could already see her
cackling and her big belly jiggling. Because my Lucienne
loved to laugh. Democritus was her master. Unbeknownst
to her, poor pet. My Lucienne never held back—she loved
to laugh. At dirty jokes, but other things too, let's be fair.
My ludic Lulu! How I adored your peals of mirth in the
silence of the night! Whatever is wrong with those people
to make them so unpleasant, I asked my friend the local
crafts scholar, who prided himself on knowing the literary gentry like the back of his hand. They're poor writers,
he said condescendingly (which irked me), and their char-
acters have been spoiled by disappointments piled atop
palinodes, stale grudges, and constant fears of disgrace.
Then I asked him who the red-faced man was, that object
of so much flattery, wheedling, and obsequious attention.

He's a bard, my friend explained, whose important function is to distribute honors and prizes to other writers. In other words, he hands out a lot of dough.

Yes? Madame Flippe? The definition of a bard? Well, think of Homer, Madame Flippe.

Any other questions?

But what a forest of hands!

Madame Basile is wondering if . . . ? No, I'm sorry, I did not have the privilege of meeting Barbara Cartland.

Madame Hardon? Is Pascal Duparc married? I have no idea, Madame Hardon. Have you any designs on that popular author?

Yes? Monsieur Bessac? Monsieur Bessac would like to know if writers favor wearing a tie. I see you have a keen interest in literary questions. There is no set rule, Monsieur Bessac. Nevertheless, it seems to me that the literary taste for untidiness does indicate a certain decline in standards.

Mademoiselle Chatterre? For those of you who did not hear, Mademoiselle Chatterre is curious to know if writers ever laugh. A most pertinent question, Mademoiselle

Chatterre. Thank you. Well, that evening, almost all of them looked as though they were attending a funeral. What did I say? Funeral? There are some words that should never pass my lips. Words that automatically send a wave of memories crashing down on me. Suddenly I see again the cemetery in the rain, so sad. The cold and empty church. Lucienne's coffin, which had to be made to measure. And into which we had serious difficulty fitting her, poor thing. As if she were hanging back from taking the great plunge. It took us several attempts to lift her body, which rigor mortis had made resistant to our maneuvers. We succeeded on the fifth try. By taking a deep breath—one, two, three, heave!—like shot-putters. Poor dear!

The way of all flesh.

I remember her elderly mama, who tried to fling herself into the grave and was unfortunately restrained. I remember the treacheries of my brother-in-law the psychiatrist, who would have led the cortege if I hadn't stepped smartly in front of him. Well, it wasn't a no-passing zone. I won't mention the wrangling over the estate, which began the very day of the interment. At the table. Again, my brother-in-law. That slanderer. After his stinging crack about belching I mentioned earlier. And another poisonous dig about the marked nature of my anal-sadistic tendencies. Meaning my venality. But I won that exchange. I'm not the sort to let myself be bested by a talking parrot.

But enough! Enough on that subject! And let us return to our Parisian soirée. Where was I? Your questions made me lose my thread. Ah, yes. The bard-dispenser of honors and prizes. I wanted to learn everything about honors and prizes. Which might come in handy some day. Is this gentlemen blessed, I inquired of my friend, with a sense of distributive justice? Absolutely, he replied. Since he conscientiously excludes every writer of merit, who might be spoiled by sudden wealth. That reply, ladies and gentlemen, left me openmouthed. And what do my colleagues think of this, I managed to ask (I remember that I said "my colleagues," I needed to create a group for myself—an old reflex!). My friend invited me to judge for myself. And we went off in opposite directions.

It didn't take me more than an hour, ladies and gentle-men, to realize that the few writers who still hoped to wangle some benefit from the bard were courting him most assiduously. As for the others, who had already abandoned their quarry, they were choking with indigna-tion, denouncing nepotism, keeping their chins up and their principles, too, discoursing on literature hand over heart and, in a lower tone, regretting their former syco-phantic behavior which had, in a way, besmirched their talent.

Madame Flippe has another question? By all means, Madame Flippe. Madame Flippe has judiciously ob-served that, on television, writers are always shown sit-ting down, which makes it impossible to tell how tall they are. That is, I agree, extremely annoying. But let us press on, if you don't mind. And return to our brilliant literary gathering.

Most of the guests, I noticed, hated one another with remarkable fervor. They aspired, legitimately, to the same renown, but since the roads to fame are narrow, they could not all crowd onto them without knocking over some fellow writer. There are quite a few collisions, it seems. Not many homicides to report, however.

Many partygoers were wary of a young author in vogue who was making a big splash among the glitterati, one Richard Montesson, a pale and silent youth who was wowing all the women.

Yes? Madame Charles? You're wondering if this prodigy is related to our druggist? I have no idea, dear Madame. What I do know, on the other hand, is that almost all the writers there that evening resented him without daring to admit it, and dreamed of his downfall while they congratulated him with sickening sweetness. Whenever they laughed, however, their merriment was chilling.

With this lecture in mind, ladies and gentlemen, I was intent on enriching and perfecting my discursive register, so after flitting from one group to another gathering impressions, I struck up a conversation with a poet who was cruising the room, suffering from a *mal de vivre* he tried in vain to shift onto others. To whom have I the pleasure of speaking? asked the poet, with an expression of nobly restrained sorrow. I gave a succinct résumé of my life and works, succinct and for good reason, wicked tongues will say. I am an author myself, I said, extending a hand that, like any true poet, he never noticed. "Seeking publisher . . . intention marriage," I added wryly, stuffing my scorned hand back into my pocket. Living, as tradition wills, off my wife Lucienne. A big eater. Suffering from serious heart failure secondary to a ponderal overload. Class A invalid. Full pension. Myself, more than sixty years of age, but youthful and enterprising of mind. Living in a town with no history, of the name of Cintegabelle, "gabelle" meaning "salt tax" and . . . But before I could finish my sentence he had turned his back on me. Had this portrait of a man blessed by life and in full possession of his art awakened his jealousy and redoubled his despair? I cannot say. The soul of a poet is unfathomable. It's been said often enough.

What conclusion can we draw today, ladies and gentlemen, from this excursion into the little world of Letters—a brief foray, admittedly, and disappointing, of course, but rich in reflections on human nature?

That it's almost impossible to talk literature to literary people. For some are busy trying to survive, the others are preoccupied with flattery, most are scandal-mongering, and they're all so enamored of their own work that they can't think of anything else.

What advice have we for those who would persist nevertheless?

These words from the good doctor, Jonathan Swift, a colleague (my little joke), who urged "conversationists," as a precaution, to steer people away from their catechisms—meaning their occupations—and to express themselves clearly without fear of appearing ordinary.

Appearing ordinary: that is the least of their worries for those who practice the conversation we shall now study:

Political Conversation.

Disillusioned by the literary world, contrary to what I had led my Lucienne to believe on my return from Paris, but that was to make myself look good, in vain as it turned out, since she was deep in a stage-four coma from which she would never emerge, disillusioned, as I was saying, by the writers of Paris, I decided to explore the political world this time around.

My friend the local writer, who has social connections, introduced me to a deputy named Letzphoque, who shortly thereafter granted me an interview in his office.

Wearing a huge pair of trousers held up by garish suspenders, this Letzphoque paced up and down with his majestic abdomen.

I asked him questions (including a few tricky ones, I admit) about the exercise of his functions. He was never caught short, waxed beautifully indignant several times, thrice uttered the word "dignity" in accents of ecstasy, patted his paunch with a satisfied hand, and lied with outstanding aplomb.

I inferred, from listening to him, that he was never so happy as when campaigning for office, when he could indulge his two favorite passions (chicanery and vote-fixing), make a hundred promises—always the same ones—with an air of determination, thrive on applause, make his voice swell whenever the word *liberty* crossed his lips, which was often, raise a glass with the voters, Here's to you, laugh heartily, give a speech that was one hundred percent retractable, slap the faithful on the back, give in to entreaties and trot out one of his famous wisecracks, about his republican opponent, a Jew, we're among friends here, and you have to have some fun, for heaven's sake, politics isn't endless tragedy.

Letzphoque, I understood, was a dangerous man.

Nevertheless it was my duty to observe, while discussing him with his closest constituents, that he was terribly persuasive. All praised his shamelessness as audacity, his trickery as shrewdness, and his vulgarity—sanctimoniously—as frankness. They found him, in a word, priceless. They were wrong. Because he knew how to extort a high price from the bounty of the nation.

From this range of evidence, I drew a few general observations which I now share with you.

The first, ladies and gentlemen, is that politicians, dedicated as they are to lies, imposture, broken promises, and rascality, transgress in the most brutal way against the splendors of conversation by shitting upon all its principles. I know, I should say that more delicately. But I'm sick and tired of being nice. And I refuse to distinguish among varying degrees of vileness.

The second remark follows from the first. The main object of political speeches is to promise everything to everyone and in the crassest manner, so deeply rooted is the conviction that too much subtlety drives the masses away. And woe to whoever dares claim that these promises are only foul deceptions. Woe to whoever insists that this system is rotten, and that we want it cleaned up. He will be accused then and there, the traitor, of hating democracy.

The final remark is that political corruption confers on its representatives an astonishing authority, since the populace credits the corrupt with a matchless capacity for deceit and for making fools of people. But is there any point in saying these things? Might the enemy profit somehow from my disillusionment?

Once I had cataloged these disappointments, ladies and gentlemen, as well as others I will spare you, for they were of the same stripe, I was inspired by a salutary

insight to compose this axiom, which comes frighten-
ingly close to revolutionary sloganeering.

—

One may deceive a people for a long time,
but one cannot delude them forever.

—

I then resolved, that very day, never to have anything
to do with politicos. On pain of winding up a terrorist.
Which would really upset me. Because I'm a timid soul.
With no idea how to handle weapons.

To keep abreast of their lies, I thought, I'll simply
watch television. That will be more than enough.

As soon as I got home, I turned on my set like a good
citizen. My only distraction since my Lulu left life for her
quietus. That word tends to make me laugh. It has a special
meaning for me. Never mind. I turned on my TV. I was in
luck. The President of the Republic was giving a speech.

Our president's last name has two angry syllables
that sound most inelegant together, the one, so to speak,
burping onto the other. Family names as ugly as that
one will bring a man down. Not our president. Who has

emerged, I must admit, unscathed. But suffers from extreme nervousness.

He spoke calmly, as befits a president, yet there was something in his face that suggested he was doing his damnedest not to curse, fume, and wing the mic out the window. Under the table he was probably holding, between two fidgety fingertips, a lighted cigarette from which he would take a deep drag the second he'd delivered his closing *Vive la France*.

The terrible effort required to repress his natural boorishness gave him that idiotic smile characteristic of penitent souls and a face as bland as his speech, yet his exertions endeared him to his audience, who kept expecting that at any moment his spring, wound too tight for too long, would snap.

While studying him, I jotted down in a notebook—absentmindedly, as often happens—the following axiom.

—

Concentration should seem a natural
part of conversation.

—

As our president's speech continued, however, I felt my thoughts slipping into melancholy. My Lulu, my light, was no longer there to interrupt his piffle every ten seconds or so by sniping at him in triumphantly bad taste. Take your finger out, she'd shout at him from the bed where she lay sprawled. And she'd crow with laughter that shook her pink flesh. For my Lucienne never could contain herself in any way. My Lucienne knew nothing, I'm serious, nothing, of the rules that govern conversation. The poor innocent. A pure child. A simple *corazón*. Me, I would keep quiet, taking advantage of those too rare moments when my Lulu was focussed on someone besides me, and I'd dream of a different life (an old habit of poets), a life without Lucienne, to be perfectly candid, a life of refinement in which conversation would be an art, and poetry an everyday thing. Blast a big fart! Lucienne would holler at the president, you'll feel better! And she'd go into gales of mirth, while motionless nearby, trying not to attract the arrow of her attention, I would invent my real life: without Lulu, or my brother-in-law the psychiatrist, that prig, or Papa, whose memory sometimes arose from the depths of my terror, or Mama, who resembled my Lulu, size-wise at least, or Tribulet, or Balin, or deputies, or publishers, or anything hurtful. Perhaps in the company of a woman, witty and ethereal, but I wasn't sure about that. Not at all sure, even. Because on the sexual plane I had reached a certain lassitude. My Lulu exhausted me, my glutton! Happy days! If I'd only known . . .

But let's not get caught in the net of regret. And let us attack with courage, we'll need it, the subject of . . .

Patriotic Conversation.

Patriotic conversation, ladies and gentlemen, is embodied, in our town, by Monsieur Tribulet, which seems absurd.

Because Monsieur Tribulet does not like to converse. Monsieur Tribulet likes only what brings in money. Well, since conversation brings in nothing, Monsieur Tribulet considers it nothing.

If I toss him an idea, Monsieur Tribulet plops it onto his scale through sheer habit. Weighing the pros and cons, he says, totting up the figures, and then he delivers his verdict. In few words, for his words are counted out, and snippily. At which point the discussion clanks to a halt or turns litigious. With intellectuals like you, he sighs. Monsieur Tribulet cannot abide intellectuals. Too arrogant. Disheveled. Always loafing under the pretext of thinking. As if that kept anyone from bustling about! No, hopeless, intellectuals. Monsieur Tribulet can't stomach them. Except those who are his customers, of course. But there aren't many. Monsieur Rêverie and myself. Not enough to support a business. At that, I speak up. My wife, I protest, eats enough for four. Ate, says Monsieur Tribulet. And realizes he has just committed a gaffe. Fix it, quick, quick. It's not house policy to contradict the clientele. It's hard, he whines, to say goodbye to those we love, and he pats my right shoulder. I'd love to elbow him right in the ribs. It's expensive, he adds. Because Monsieur Tribulet counts his feelings the way he counts his cash.

Today Monsieur Tribulet is in good form. He talks. He enjoyed the President of the Republic's speech on the eight-o'clock news. Monsieur Tribulet is on the barricades for his principles and on his knees before the president. Monsieur Tribulet kneels before all the presidents of the Republic. And Monsieur Tribulet is a patriot, too: he frequently looks grumpy.

—

Patriotic feelings often lead to grumpiness.

—

Since a grumpy face is taboo in conversation,

—

you won't get far with a
patriotic subject of conversation.

—

Still, I persevere. I love talking about my country. I can't help it. Love of country is beyond our control. It arrives. We welcome it. So it is with all love. Since Monsieur Tribulet is the person whom I encounter most routinely in this world (a lot less, it's true, than when my Lulu was alive), he is the one with whom I share my perplexities about France. Cold comfort.

All France's misfortunes, I tell him, stem from the idea that we are an important country. We are, thunders Monsieur Tribulet. And yet, I say, our rivers, if we measure them, are piss-streams, our mountains, compared to peaks in the Orient, are hillocks, our . . . Stop right there, shouts Tribulet. Why should I? I reply. We glare at one another. All joking aside, how much do you want? asks Monsieur Tribulet. Two-hundred-and-fifty grams, I answer; four times less than before, I tell him, suddenly sad. And speaking of downsizing, it's high time, I say, that our poor France recover a sense of proportion and take a courageous look at what's gone wrong. And you know, do you, what's gone wrong? ripostes Monsieur Tribulet sarcastically. Three hundred grams! Is that all right? Perfect, I say. Certain bastards, I tell him, are urging our France to lower her standards, which has already happened, and if this decline continues France will end up . . . Anything else? cuts in Monsieur Tribulet.

Because Monsieur Tribulet cannot abide chitchat. It gives him a bellyache. Gets on his nerves. And if you keep it up, he might have a tantrum. He can't afford to screw around all day, good God almighty! Nobody's paying him to stand there doing nothing! He's not talking about you, of course. He has only the greatest respect for retirees. But talking for talking's sake, no, he can't, his work ethic is too strong, what can you do! Anyway, politics doesn't interest him. Monsieur Tribulet, in case you didn't know, is absolutely apolitical.

—

Patriotic conversations with Monsieur Tribulet
usually turn sour.

—

Three days ago, Monsieur Tribulet was extremely displeased. It showed in his face. Something about a stolen car radio.

Monsieur Tribulet is often displeased. His displeasure fills in for his political opinions. But Monsieur Tribulet has figured out how to exorcise his displeasure. Get rid of the bêtes noires! They occupy all his thoughts. They occupy all his space. Black cats? I ask, feigning surprise. He shrugs. Don't pretend to be more of an ass than you are already! he snaps. And since it's not my style to concede defeat to the likes of Monsieur Tribulet, I reply with this sentence lifted from the Psalms, which leaves him tongue-tied.

—

Whosoever loves iniquity is the enemy of his soul.

—

And since I've just disposed of Monsieur Tribulet, at least temporarily, I will now speak to you about a conversation of which I have become the herald, a

Conversation with the Dead.

I've saved the best for last, a conversation I engage in—without exaggeration—from dawn to dusk and all the days God made, with my Lucienne, and I think I can speak with some authority here, with my Lucienne who began talking to me on the evening of January 2, 1999, and hasn't stopped since, sometimes she makes me dizzy, but far be it from me to complain, because once I got over the initial shock, our conversation attained a kind of perfection, our conversation has become ideal, because our dead ends and our failures, ladies and gentlemen, which I have confided to you throughout this lecture and which I described as hopeless, were not in vain. Through mighty death, my Lulu has become polite to the point of self-effacement, humble without servility, restrained, forbearing, and gracious, because the dead, ladies and gentlemen, are free of prejudice and open to all discourse—amorous, literary, political, and patriotic: their conversation subsumes all others, to put it elegantly. Through mighty death, my Lulu has become as meek as a lamb, because the dead, ladies and gentlemen, are as meek as lambs, it's common knowledge, the dead, ladies and gentlemen, wouldn't hurt a fly. And ever since my Lulu learned the vanity of all things, she has detached herself from incidental pleasures, she eats nothing, she subsists on my words alone, because the dead, ladies and gentlemen, live solely on the words of the living, which is valuable to know, and those who have no one to talk to die a second death, so if, as I fear, conversation is disappearing, our dead, all our dead, ladies and gentlemen, will disappear, I can promise you, since by dying, conversation will kill off our dead, because the dead, I insist, live on our words, and vice versa, what I mean is that we the living live on the speech of our dead, which is a hundred times better than we are, I myself live, my dear, on your words that reach me haloed in silence, like a religious experience, that's what I tried to explain to your brother the psychiatrist who stared at me as though I were crazy, I told him that you were teaching me, day after day, my Lulu, a thousand things: that one may live in the darkness without fearing it, that indifference is a strength (yours astounds me), that the eternity where you lie gives you a patience and a wisdom I hope to emulate, What's the point of working yourself to death? you whisper to me from the heart of your silence, why suffer from toiling through life when it's so short? Push sorrow away, you order me, it breeds bad thoughts. Take advantage of life, seize hold of it, enjoy it, you murmur to me, and other such things that do me a world of good and that I am happy, ladies and gentlemen, to pass on to you.

As you can see, I'm ending my lecture with a flourish. I say "ending," not "concluding," since to come to a conclusion is the mark of an ass, as Gustave used to say, a cousin of mine, I'm kidding. Because the time has come for us to part. Ferdinand informs me that it's nine-thirty. Closing time. So what shall I tell you in closing, my dear friends of Cintegabelle? I will simply give you the following advice. Put on your coats, because it's cold outside. Leave the town hall. Walk briskly along the Rue Fayol. Until you come to the Avenue du Général-Leclerc. Turn left. And enter the Café des Ormes. With or without your dead. I'll await you there. For some conversation. It's the only way to stand our ground.

See you in a few minutes.

SOME NOTES ON THE TRANSLATION

The Cintegabelle Lecture is a book that speaks for itself: allusive, astringent, comic, digressive, ironic, mordant, pungent, vituperative—the narrative voice is endlessly variable. (And very, very tricky, from a translator's point of view.) Not a great deal happens in this novel, but the language is certainly busy: our lecturer's *mano a mano* with what comes out of his own mouth is the closest thing to a plot the reader will find, overshadowing even the mysterious demise of the cetaceous Lucienne. The shifting currents of slang, formality, erudition, vulgarity, wisdom, idiocy, and what-have-you give the text a quicksilver sheen, and the seeker after meaning here may feel, like the ancient captors of Proteus, that the truth just won't stay put.

I have tried to make the sea change from French to English as deft as possible, but some things always slip through the net, or cannot survive removal from their native habitat. When I encountered some particularly French cultural tidbit, I sometimes added a word or two of explanation: Adamo was a "teenage crooner," for example, and Fénelon a "philosopher Archbishop," while the political tenor of Gracq's lampoon, familiar to Lydie Salvayre's French readership, was labeled "anti-consumerism." I identified Michaux's imaginary Bordètes as such, but left Baltasar Gracián (1601-1658, the Spanish author of *The Art of Worldly Wisdom*) alone. Many readers might see Madame de Sévigné in "*la Marquise*," and know only one "Gustave," Flaubert. The pesky Tribulet sounds suspiciously like Triboulet, the evil court jester in Victor Hugo's play, *Le Roi s'amuse*, which inspired Verdi's opera *Rigoletto*. Naughtily evocative, a few other French names morphed into English counterparts, like Madame Durtut (*dur tout*; hard all; all hard; Hardon), or the politician, Bezons (*baisons*; let's fuck; Letzphoque). The literal meaning of one name, Monsieur Songe, was too lovely to lose, so he became Monsieur Rêverie, but those familiar with modern French literature will now recognize a reference to the Monsieur Songe of the novelist Robert Pinget.

Lucienne, "my Muse, my sacrificed Mumuse," occasioned one bit of choice wordplay I could not wrangle into English: *faire mumuse* means "to toy with," "not to be serious about." For those readers who noticed that the immovable Lucienne, who lived with her husband in Cintegabelle, somehow managed to die in her birthplace, Fatarella, here is the author's explanation: "From book to book, my 'heroines' are born and die in Fatarella, which is actually my mother's native village. So it's a purely arbitrary thing." A psychiatrist who practices in Toulouse, Lydie Salvayre was born in France to refugees from the Spanish Civil War: her mother was an anarchist, her father a communist. Make of that what you will.

And if your Latin is rusty, *Bonum vinum laetificat cor hominis* means "Good wine delights the heart of man"—a sterling sentiment, and a fine exit line.

—

p. 66, l. 3	A reference to Uncle Toby and Corporal Trim in Laurence Sterne's *Tristram Shandy*.
p. 120, l. 18	Jacques Chirac: "Chi" recalls chier, "to shit," as "rac" does raquer, "to fork over," "cough up," as in extortion.

LINDA COVERDALE

ABOUT THE AUTHOR

Lydie Salvayre, the daughter of refugees from the Spanish Civil War, grew up in the south of France where she attended medical school and received a degree in psychiatry. It wasn't until she was in her mid-forties that she published her first novel, *The Declaration*. Since that time she has published nine other books, including *Everyday Life*, *The Company of Ghosts*, *Some Useful Advice for Apprentice Process Servers*, and *The Power of Flies*, all of which are forthcoming from Dalkey Archive Press. She has received numerous accolades and awards in France for her fiction, including the Prix Hermes for *The Declaration*, and the Prix Novembre for *The Company of Ghosts*.

SELECTED DALKEY ARCHIVE PAPERBACKS

CAROLE MASO, *AVA*.

LADISLAV MATEJKA AND KRYSTYNA POMORSKA, EDS., *Readings in Russian Poetics: Formalist and Structuralist Views*.

HARRY MATHEWS, *The Case of the Persevering Maltese: Collected Essays*.
Cigarettes.
The Conversions.
The Human Country: New and Collected Stories.
The Journalist.
My Life in CIA.
Singular Pleasures.
The Sinking of the Odradek Stadium.
Tlooth.
20 Lines a Day.

ROBERT L. MCLAUGHLIN, ED., *Innovations: An Anthology of Modern & Contemporary Fiction*.

STEVEN MILLHAUSER, *The Barnum Museum*.
In the Penny Arcade.

RALPH J. MILLS, JR., *Essays on Poetry*.

OLIVE MOORE, *Spleen*.

NICHOLAS MOSLEY, *Accident*.
Assassins.
Catastrophe Practice.
Children of Darkness and Light.
The Hesperides Tree.
Hopeful Monsters.
Imago Bird.
Impossible Object.
Inventing God.
Judith.
Natalie Natalia.
Serpent.
The Uses of Slime Mould: Essays of Four Decades.

WARREN F. MOTTE, JR., *Fables of the Novel: French Fiction since 1990*.
Oulipo: A Primer of Potential Literature.

YVES NAVARRE, *Our Share of Time*.

DOROTHY NELSON, *Tar and Feathers*.

WILFRIDO D. NOLLEDO, *But for the Lovers*.

FLANN O'BRIEN, *At Swim-Two-Birds*.
At War.
The Best of Myles.
The Dalkey Archive.
Further Cuttings.
The Hard Life.
The Poor Mouth.
The Third Policeman.

CLAUDE OLLIER, *The Mise-en-Scène*.

PATRIK OUŘEDNÍK, *Europeana*.

FERNANDO DEL PASO, *Palinuro of Mexico*.

ROBERT PINGET, *The Inquisitory*.
Mahu or The Material.

RAYMOND QUENEAU, *The Last Days*.
Odile.
Pierrot Mon Ami.
Saint Glinglin.

ANN QUIN, *Berg*.
Passages.
Three.
Tripticks.

ISHMAEL REED, *The Free-Lance Pallbearers*.
The Last Days of Louisiana Red.
Reckless Eyeballing.
The Terrible Threes.
The Terrible Twos.
Yellow Back Radio Broke-Down.

JULIÁN RÍOS, *Larva: A Midsummer Night's Babel*.
Poundemonium.

AUGUSTO ROA BASTOS, *I the Supreme*.

JACQUES ROUBAUD, *The Great Fire of London*.
Hortense in Exile.
Hortense Is Abducted.
The Plurality of Worlds of Lewis.
The Princess Hoppy.
Some Thing Black.

LEON S. ROUDIEZ, *French Fiction Revisited*.

VEDRANA RUDAN, *Night*.

LYDIE SALVAYRE, *The Lecture*.

LUIS RAFAEL SÁNCHEZ, *Macho Camacho's Beat*.

SEVERO SARDUY, *Cobra & Maitreya*.

NATHALIE SARRAUTE, *Do You Hear Them?*
Martereau.

ARNO SCHMIDT, *Collected Stories*.
Nobodaddy's Children.

CHRISTINE SCHUTT, *Nightwork*.

GAIL SCOTT, *My Paris*.

JUNE AKERS SEESE, *Is This What Other Women Feel Too?*
What Waiting Really Means.

AURELIE SHEEHAN, *Jack Kerouac Is Pregnant*.

VIKTOR SHKLOVSKY, *Knight's Move*.
A Sentimental Journey: Memoirs 1917-1922.
Theory of Prose.
Third Factory.
Zoo, or Letters Not about Love.

JOSEF ŠKVORECKÝ, *The Engineer of Human Souls*.

CLAUDE SIMON, *The Invitation*.

GILBERT SORRENTINO, *Aberration of Starlight*.
Blue Pastoral.
Crystal Vision.
Imaginative Qualities of Actual Things.
Mulligan Stew.
Pack of Lies.
The Sky Changes.
Something Said.
Splendide-Hôtel.
Steelwork.
Under the Shadow.

W. M. SPACKMAN, *The Complete Fiction*.

GERTRUDE STEIN, *Lucy Church Amiably*.
The Making of Americans.
A Novel of Thank You.

PIOTR SZEWC, *Annihilation*.

STEFAN THEMERSON, *Tom Harris*.

JEAN-PHILIPPE TOUSSAINT, *Television*.

ESTHER TUSQUETS, *Stranded*.

DUBRAVKA UGRESIC, *Lend Me Your Character*.
Thank You for Not Reading.

LUISA VALENZUELA, *He Who Searches*.

BORIS VIAN, *Heartsnatcher*.

PAUL WEST, *Words for a Deaf Daughter & Gala*.

CURTIS WHITE, *America's Magic Mountain*.
The Idea of Home.
Memories of My Father Watching TV.
Monstrous Possibility: An Invitation to Literary Politics.
Requiem.

DIANE WILLIAMS, *Excitability: Selected Stories*.
Romancer Erector.

DOUGLAS WOOLF, *Wall to Wall*.
Ya! & John-Juan.

PHILIP WYLIE, *Generation of Vipers*.

MARGUERITE YOUNG, *Angel in the Forest*.
Miss MacIntosh, My Darling.

REYOUNG, *Unbabbling*.

LOUIS ZUKOFSKY, *Collected Fiction*.

SCOTT ZWIREN, *God Head*.

FOR A FULL LIST OF PUBLICATIONS, VISIT:
www.dalkeyarchive.com